I0557354

VESTA EXILED

STERLING R. WALKER

Vesta Exiled
©2018 Sterling R. Walker

Cover by Jessica Phillips
Models: Jared Weaver, Jayden Beach, Aaron Weaver

Printed in the United States of America

ISBN 13: 978-0-9900190-7-7
ISBN 10: 0990019071

Science Fiction/Young Adult
Second Edition
1 2 3 4 5 6 7 8 9 10

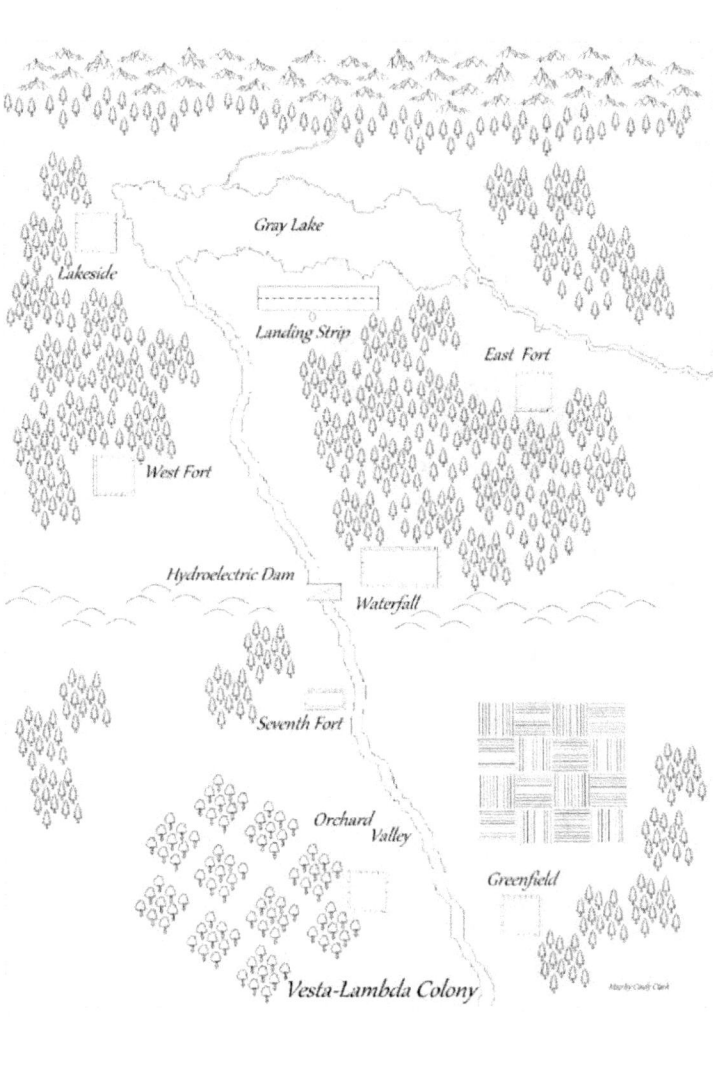

Gray Lake

Lakeside

Landing Strip

East Fort

West Fort

Hydroelectric Dam

Waterfall

Seventh Fort

Orchard Valley

Greenfield

Vesta-Lambda Colony

Map by Cindy Clark

ONE
STRAY

"Eliana's in labor!" Solona announced, bursting through the front door.

Nikki shrieked and fell off the chair she was using to reach the latches on the kitchen window. "It's too early, Mom! The baby's not due for three weeks!"

Her mother dropped a bucket next to the door, along with the trowel and spade she used to harvest herbs from the rooftop garden. She ran to the kitchen to scrub her dirt-encrusted fingernails at the sink. "The sudden change in air pressure probably started her contractions. Derek told me they're already at the hospital ship."

"But the storm's about to break!" Nikki scrambled to her feet. "We can't go outside now!"

"We'll have to run like a night terror's on our heels." Solona grabbed her backpack filled with herbal remedies from a lower cabinet. "Let's go!"

"But don't we need to take food—supplies—?" Nikki sputtered protests as she hopped up and down on one foot, then the other, pulling on her waterproof bluedeer-skin boots. "We'll be stuck

1

inside the ship for three days—if we make it there alive!"

"Don't be so dramatic. We'll be safer in the ship than we are here. Plenty of food and water and beds." Her mother was out the door before Nikki finished tying her second boot.

Nikki locked the door to their tiny apartment and ran to catch up with her mother. They lived on the second floor of Lakeside's south fortress wall, so it was a short dash down one flight of stairs and a twenty-meter sprint to the gates.

The streets were abandoned, every door and window boarded up in anticipation of the annual storm. The torrential rains would overflow the gutters, turning the cobblestone streets into canals. The wind was already gusting hard, plastering Nikki's clothes to her body, whipping her dark hair across her eyes, and pelting her face with leaves and debris.

Two sentries at the gates struggled against the wind to pull the tall doors shut as Solona and Nikki slipped by, racing beneath the archway to exit Lakeside. One of the sentries shouted at them, but Nikki couldn't hear anything over the howling wind. She assumed he was warning her they didn't have enough time to make it to the landing strip on foot, and they wouldn't be able to get back inside the fort with the gates closed.

"Who's being dramatic?" she shouted at her mother's back. "This is suicide!"

Solona eyed Nikki over her shoulder, but her response was drowned out by a *boom* of thunder.

Let's pray we don't get struck by lightning. Nikki grimaced and kept running.

The path bordering the shoreline of Gray Lake was two kilometers long. Normally an easy twenty-minute walk to the landing strip, it took them twice as long to navigate the obstacle course of falling branches and panicked wildlife scurrying for cover. By the time they reached the opposite side of the lake and the wide bridge which spanned the Cold River, Nikki was clutching at a stitch in her side.

"Hurry!" New worry lines etched her mother's sweaty face. "Derek said she's fully dilated!"

Nikki envied her brother-in-law's Talent. Sending thoughts to someone else's mind was a useful skill, especially since news traveled slowly now that Vesta colony's communication devices had worn out.

The landing strip was on the other side of the bridge. Nineteen massive starships were parked permanently on both sides of the tarmac, their rusting metal carcasses forming a village, of sorts. It was a ghost town most colonists avoided unless weather or a medical emergency forced them to pay a visit.

Halfway across the concrete span of the bridge, Nikki glanced down at the choppy gray water choked with tree branches and debris. The broken boards from a clothesline floated by, the remains of someone's laundry tangled in the wires.

The first ship past the bridge had once been named after a famous Earth leader, but no one alive recalled who it was. Now it was simply referred to as the Shrine. Nikki always got a chill down her spine whenever she passed the sealed-off ramp to the massive, silver, bird-shaped craft. Vines obscured the landing pods, underbelly, and most of the first level from view, but the sign carved into a smooth round stone at the foot of the gangway was always kept clear of vegetation.

First Ship
Dedicated to the
Vesta-Lambda Colony Plague Victims
Twelfth month, VA 69
Rest in Peace
Danger—No Entrance

Nikki ignored the cold, sick feeling in the pit of her stomach as she increased her pace to catch up with her mother. Weeds, briars, and curling vines grew up through hundreds of cracks in the crumbling tarmac which separated the Shrine from their destination, the last ship. Smaller and less rusty than the other ships, it served as the colony's hospital.

She reached the foot of the gangway and glanced up at the circular door of the outer airlock. Solona was already at the top of the ramp, tapping the public entry code into the keypad to the right of the door. By the time Nikki reached her side, the airlock had opened.

They stepped inside, and the round door rotated shut behind them, cutting off the punishing winds and most of the noise from the thunder.

"Ms. Zegarelli! I'm glad you made it!" A young dark-skinned woman Nikki didn't recognize rushed forward to greet them. She wore a nurse's lab coat which used to be white, but now was a washed-out gray dotted with faded pink bloodstains.

"Are you on duty alone today, Yasmin?" Solona asked.

The young woman nodded, wide-eyed. "Right this way—hurry."

Nikki followed her mother and Yasmin up the ship's central ladder to the third level.

"Eliana's in the surgical room." The nurse led them down a short, narrow corridor.

"Surgery?" Solona's high-pitched reply surprised Nikki. She didn't realize her mother was nervous.

"In case the baby needs to be resuscitated," Yasmin explained over her shoulder. "We're down to the last oxygen tank."

"Last tank?" Solona repeated. "Darkness. How can a colony survive sixteen storms without new medical supplies?"

"I don't know, ma'am," Yasmin said.

"You'll have to excuse Mom," Nikki said. "It's her first grandchild."

"I understand." Yasmin ushered them into a small room which reeked of antiseptic air.

"Elie!" Solona rushed to her eldest daughter's side.

Nikki hung back in the doorway, not wanting to crowd her sister and her husband Derek, who hovered at Eliana's other side. Yasmin and Solona barely had enough room to attend the mother-to-be.

Eliana's normally peaches-and-cream complexion was now bright red to match her long, tangled hair. She sat upright, legs wide apart, in a specialized birthing bed which supported her thighs, allowing her to concentrate on pushing.

As an apprentice herbalist, Nikki had assisted at a few births, but it was daunting to witness her reserved, soft-spoken sister transformed into something primeval. Eliana was naked and howling obscenities.

Solona went to work, rubbing oils on Eliana's huge belly and whispering encouragement whenever she stopped screeching long enough to gasp for breath.

Derek was pale beneath his dark complexion, his coarse black crew cut gleaming with perspiration. He stroked Eliana's shoulder in a distracted way, looking close to losing his lunch.

"Send her good thoughts," Nikki said.

"I am." Derek regarded Nikki, offered a queasy smile, and returned his attention to the tiny head beginning to crown.

"I—am—never—doing—this—again!" Eliana bellowed before focusing on one last mighty push.

Remind her she said that, next time she says she wants to have a baby. Derek's voice in Nikki's mind sounded surprisingly calm.

Solona's skilled hands were ready to guide the slippery body into the world. She lifted the newborn and placed him on Eliana's chest. He immediately cried, even as his mother breathed a loud sigh of relief.

"It's a boy!" Yasmin had been eager to have a more-experienced nurse take over the delivery, but now she sprang into action, placing a warm blanket over the baby and clamping the umbilical cord. "Congratulations!"

Mother, father, and grandmother huddled over the bawling bundle of joy while Nikki kept her distance.

After fifteen minutes of admiring newborn Travis, Eliana glanced over at Nikki with a weary smile. "Do you want to hold him?"

"I can't." Hot tears stung the corners of Nikki's eyes, but she blinked them away, hoping no one noticed. "You know I can't."

"He's a newborn. There won't be any memories. Come on," Solona said when Nikki shook her head again. "Just try. It'll be fine."

A knot of fear formed in Nikki's stomach as she crossed the small room to join the crowd at Eliana's bedside. Solona stepped back to make space for her.

Travis was pink and squashed-looking, like a lump of bread dough with eyes. He had stopped crying and was gazing at his mother's face. Nikki suspected his wild, damp hair would be auburn like Eliana's when it dried.

Nikki extended an index finger and touched the back of the baby's tiny fist. The images that filled her mind were gentle and blurry, with an ethereal, dream-like quality. Solona was right, Travis had no concrete memories, only snippets of emotions, mostly happy ones.

"Hold him." Eliana offered a smile of encouragement.

Nikki had never held an infant before, never had physical contact with anyone, really, for more than a few seconds. The knot in her stomach tightened, but her sister put Travis in her arms before she could refuse.

Two remarkable things happened as Nikki held her nephew and he gazed up at her with alert eyes. First, she felt a spark of hope that the Talent she struggled to understand wasn't a curse but had a real purpose. It could be useful if she learned how to master it. Second, she sensed Travis possessed a Talent similar to hers, but more powerful.

"He's a Stray," she whispered.

"What?" Eliana gasped. "Are you sure?"

"I'm positive." The images from the baby's mind left hers the moment she relinquished him to Derek's waiting arms. "But I have no idea what his Talent is," she added before anyone asked her to explain.

"There're only a handful of second-generation Strays in the colony," Solona said, "but I'm sure the number will grow now that all the Strays are adults. It'll be interesting to see their Talents emerge."

"Interesting?" A crease formed between Derek's thick black eyebrows. "The Survivors already treat us like we have the Plague. How're they going to treat our children?"

"I don't know." Solona's grim expression mirrored Derek's. "But let's not worry about it today. Right now I just want to hold my grandson."

A deafening *boom* echoed outside the ship. The skies opened up, and rain lashed the room's tiny port window.

I guess you'll get to hold him a lot for the next few days, Mom.

TWO
STORM

"I'm thinking of changing careers." Corban Abrams shouted to be heard over the rhythmic clanging of hammers on anvils.

"You're only seventeen. You don't have a career." Corban's brother Thane took a smoking rectangle from the coals with long-handled tongs and set to work shaping the molten iron on his anvil with practiced blows from his flatter.

"I want to change guilds," Corban shouted.

Thane raised the visor of his welding mask, revealing a sweaty scowl. "Are you crazy?" He set the flatter down and dipped the glowing metal into the water. He gave Corban his full attention as the bucket emitted clouds of steam. "Uncle will never let you leave the hunters."

"You left." Corban knew it was tactless, but the words slipped out.

"It's hard to track bluedeer when you're missing a kneecap." Thane kept his temper in check, but the dangerous expression on his face warned Corban to shut his mouth.

9

"Sorry." The response was automatic, as was his glance down at Thane's left knee. A titanium brace encased his denim pant leg, taking his weight off the mangled calf and knee joint. The device was a poor substitute for a prosthetic knee, but Thane was fortunate to have a brace at all. Being the mayor's nephew did have its privileges. Anyone else in West Fort with a similar injury would be forced to make do with a wooden leg.

A night terror attack eight storms ago was the reason for the brace. Thane's legs were thin, but as a metal-smith's apprentice, he was solid muscle from the waist up. Long blond hair and patchy beard, both in need of a trim, framed Thane's prominent cheekbones and blue eyes.

"Assuming Uncle lets you change guilds—and we both know it's never going to happen—which one are you thinking of?" With his right hand, Thane selected a round punch hammer and reached, with his left, for the tongs immersed in the bucket.

"Medics."

Thane snorted with laughter. "I thought you were going to say you wanted to be a songwriter. Can you imagine the look on Uncle's face if you told him you wanted to join the artists?"

Corban didn't crack a smile at Thane's lame attempt at humor.

Thane sobered and shoved the tongs back into the coals. "Why the medics?"

"I don't like hunting."

"I didn't think you were squeamish."

"I'm not. You know blood doesn't bother me. I just don't like killing. I'd rather put bodies back together instead of tear them apart." Corban eyed

Thane's leg again, for emphasis. "You could convince Uncle to hear me out."

Thane frowned, skeptical. "He'll never agree to let you switch. You'll have to wait until you're eighteen." He lowered his visor and went back to work, pounding screw holes into the almost finished door hinge.

Corban blew out a breath of frustration and turned to leave the shed, passing the workstations of the other three apprentice metal-smiths, who ignored him.

Outside, the morning air was chilly compared to the stifling heat of the smithy, even though the temperature on Vesta never dipped below 25° C. Corban made an effort to cool his temper, as well as his body, as he threaded the maze of makeshift market stalls, walking toward Main Street. Sleepy vendors were setting up for the day's business.

Past the pottery kiln, Corban reached the road and turned left, heading toward West Fort Community School. If he hurried, he would be fifteen minutes late for his first class. He raced along the narrow street between row houses, watching where he placed his feet so he wouldn't turn an ankle on the uneven cobblestones.

A glace upward to estimate the time made him stop in his tracks.

Iron-gray clouds were rolling in from the mountains, blotting out the warm pink glow of Ilios. It was a warning that the annual storm was gathering.

***

11

The West Fort colonists worked fast to prepare for the storm. The community water system and solar electric grid were the first things to be shut down. Since four hundred families lived in the apartments that formed the fortress walls and in the crowded courtyard village, turning off the water created a huge demand for the hand pumps. People rushed to fill buckets until it was time to cover the wells with large stones to keep out debris.

Colonists secured the shutters over every window and exterior door, distributed all the food in the dining hall, and filled clay lamps with enough flaxseed oil to burn for three days. Sometimes the storm lasted four days. Corban didn't want to think about riding out a four-day storm.

"Are you sure you don't want to take shelter in one of the ships this time?" Thane asked when the brothers reached their apartment, with arms loaded with food and supplies.

Corban shook his head. "I'm not bunking with strangers. We'll be fine here." It was the same argument every storm, but he refused to leave his handicapped brother alone to fend for himself.

Thane grunted something which could be interpreted as a "thank you," but Corban dismissed it with a shrug. He took their hammocks down from the log walls and carried them to the three-by-three meter windowless bathroom which served as their storm shelter. He hung the hammocks from the eyehooks screwed into the stone walls.

Corban secured the wooden toilet lid, grateful they lived on the third floor of the fort. The outdated septic system sometimes flooded from the relentless rains, leaving the first floor residents knee-deep in raw sewage.

Thane placed their food rations and eating utensils on the sink counter. He frowned at the results. "I don't think we can live off a bowl of bluedeer jerky, two loaves of bread, and six plums."

Corban picked up a plum and started to take a bite.

"Wait!" Thane snatched the fruit from his hand. "We're going to need that."

"I didn't have any breakfast."

"Neither did I, but it'll have to wait. See if Uncle has any food stashed in the kitchen." Thane set the plum on the counter. "This is off-limits until tonight."

Fear washed over Corban at the thought of sneaking into their uncle's domain, but he didn't want his brother to think he was a coward. "Sure, I can do that."

Thane closed his eyes for a moment, concentrating his Talent. "I don't hear him in the apartment." He gave Corban a nod of reassurance. "You'd better hurry. The storm's about to break."

Corban crossed their small bedroom to the door that adjoined the mayor's suite. He knocked once, out of habit, before poking his head inside his uncle's bedroom. The room was unoccupied, as Thane reported, but Corban sensed the need for caution.

A huge bed, covered with a beautiful quilt and real down-filled pillows, took up most of the room. Several fine-woven suits in assorted colors hung in the corner wardrobe. The mayor also enjoyed his own private bathroom with expensive copper fixtures. It was quite a contrast from the wooden privy the brothers shared.

Corban peeked into the next room. Leighton Abrams's spacious sitting room had been converted into a meeting space for the community council. A kitchenette flanked one wall and a long oval table surrounded by seven matching chairs filled the center of the room. Soft white night terror fur rugs covered the floor.

Taking a deep breath, Corban went straight to the refrigerator and opened the door. He surveyed the contents in astonishment. *Tangerines? Asparagus? Hardboiled eggs? Is that goat cheese? Where did Leighton get all this?* He ignored his guilty conscience and filled his pockets. *Why shouldn't we help ourselves? The power is off so everything will spoil before the storm's over.*

"Where did all this come from?" Corban asked himself.

"Where did *what* come from?" a cold voice behind him asked.

"Uncle!" Corban spun around, clutching a hand to his heart from the shock. "Darkness! I didn't hear you come in!"

The mayor appraised his nephew with a suspicious frown. He was a tall man, but height was the only physical feature he shared with Thane and Corban. Leighton Abrams's skin was pale, in sharp contrast to his jet-black hair and dark gray eyes. Streaks of silver accentuated the hair at his temples and in his bushy black eyebrows. The mayor carried himself as one who knew how to wield authority with a heavy hand.

"I was looking for a few extra supplies for the storm." Corban's resolve faltered under his uncle's malevolent stare. He figured it was easier to confess than to endure a hostile interrogation.

14

But Leighton didn't question him further. Corban sensed his uncle's anger spiraling out of control. "So now you're a *thief* as well as a *liar*?"

The words stung, but Corban was used to the verbal abuse. He opened his mouth to defend himself, but before he uttered a word, his uncle seized him by the shoulders and slammed his back against the open refrigerator.

A ceramic jar filled with wine fell off a shelf and shattered at their feet.

"Now look what you've done!" The mayor dragged Corban away from the fridge and shoved him toward the door. "Get out!"

Without a word, Corban fled the suite, leaving a trail of wine footprints behind. He was accustomed to his uncle's explosive temper, but as a minor under colonial law, he had no recourse but to endure it until he was eighteen. Running away wasn't an option on Vesta.

There was nowhere to run.

When Corban reached the bathroom/storm shelter, Thane looked up from the rain barrel he was setting in the corner. "I'm sorry! I didn't hear him coming upstairs until you were already at the fridge."

Corban made an effort to wipe the scowl off his face. "Forget it. He was already mad about something. It was bad timing." He emptied his pockets of a handful of asparagus, four tangerines, and six hardboiled eggs. "Darkness. I hope this was worth getting caught. Where does Uncle get all this stuff?" He sat on the toilet lid and took off his soaked socks.

"He trades for it." Thane threw him a towel to blot up the puddle of wine. "You might want to put some dry clothes on before we barricade the door."

"Trades what? He hasn't gone hunting since he was elected." Corban returned to the bedroom to grab some jeans and socks from his dresser. He didn't care if the wine footprints stained his uncle's precious hardwood floors and left his wet clothes right where he shed them. He returned to the bathroom as soon as he was dressed.

Thane continued their conversation. "Uncle trades favors."

Corban groaned. "You mean he's taking bribes?"

His brother shot him an astonished look. "You didn't know?"

"You didn't tell me."

Thane shrugged. "I don't repeat everything I overhear because, one, not much is worth repeating, and two, you usually know before I open my mouth."

"I didn't know about this. I'm not telepathic."

"No, but you're empathic, so that's close enough." Thane shook his head. "I feel sorry for any Stray who can read minds. I'm sure what goes on in people's heads is worse than what comes out of their mouths."

The first rumblings of thunder brought their banter to a halt. Corban lit the lamp and set it on the floor.

Thane placed the heavy iron bar across the door to secure it. "Did you bring the cards?"

"Yes." Corban searched his cargo pockets for the faded deck they used during the storms. The brothers sat on the floor and played a game of Spades.

The wind began to howl. They exchanged a look of resignation; it would get louder over the next few days.

They played cards for several hours to the continuous roar of the wind and thunder, like a giant beast clawing at the stone walls of the fort.

Corban did his best to ignore the forces of nature raging outside their tiny room. The hours crawled by as the storm lashed Vesta. The brothers ate, napped, played cards, ate, and slept again. They extinguished the lamp to conserve oil when they went to sleep, but the pitch darkness made Corban uneasy. *A storm shelter must be terrifying for someone with claustrophobia.*

It was impossible to tell if it was night or day outside. They ate when they were hungry and slept when they were tired. Because it wasn't safe to uncover the toilet, they used a chamber pot. It had a lid but didn't contain all the odors.

"I've got to have some fresh air," Corban said.

"There's enough small gaps in these stones to keep us from suffocating." Thane took off the brace and used his good leg to hoist himself into his hammock.

Corban stretched out in his own hammock and shut his eyes.

***

He awoke with a gasp of horror and sat up. His hammock capsized, dumped him onto the hard wooden floor, and knocked the wind out of him. He remained on the floor for a few minutes, shivering at the fresh perspiration that drenched his torso. Corban took some deep breaths to slow his racing heart.

The storm had reached fever pitch, the thunder like intermittent explosions outside their shelter. Static electricity charged the air, making Corban's hair stand on end. He was envious of Thane, sound asleep in the other hammock. His brother didn't pause in his snores because his Talent allowed him to tune in or tune out sounds at will.

Corban climbed to his unsteady feet, rubbing his bruised hip. He picked up the blanket, eased himself back into the hammock, and pulled the cover up to his shoulders to ward off the chill. He was tired, but unable to go back to sleep. He had enough experience with his own Talent to know he should analyze the nightmare while the images were still fresh in his mind.

In the dream, he was standing in a grove of fruit trees covered with pink blossoms, fifteen kilometers to the south near Orchard Valley fortress. He identified peach pits in the weeds beneath his feet. In the distance, he saw a young woman running toward him through the trees. She was dressed in blue jeans and a long-sleeved black T-shirt smeared with blood, and she had a long sword in her right hand.

Corban recognized the sword. Thane had forged it a few months ago as a gift for their uncle on his fiftieth birthday.

The stranger came straight at Corban, full speed. He noted the hatred in her expression. He knew he should take cover, or at least get out of her way, but his feet were frozen to the ground. Somehow he knew her, although he never set eyes on her before the dream, and somehow he wasn't afraid of this enraged person who appeared intent on killing him right where he stood.

Her features burned an image into his memory. The top of her head was level with his chin, making her at least 1.8 meters. She was tan but not too dark, like someone who worked outside all day. Her large brown eyes slanted upward at the outside corners, and her black hair was long and coming loose from its ponytail. A few stray curls clung to her forehead and the edges of her flushed face.

The entire package was attractive but terrifying. Terror flooded Corban as she raised the sword over her head in both hands and swung it downward in a vicious arch, aiming right for his neck.

This was the moment he had been wrenched from sleep with a gasp of horror.

Corban's heart hammered against his ribs. He raised a hand to his sweaty throat, assuring himself his head was still in place. In the dream, the blade came so close he felt the edge against his neck.

What does it mean? Corban's premonitions sometimes showed him scenes so far into the future, it was impossible to relate them to what was currently going on in his life. They offered him glimpses of upcoming events, but important details were always missing, like a puzzle without all the pieces.

Who is she? Why does she have Uncle's sword? Why does she want to kill me? As with most of his premonitions, this one needed to be placed on a wait-and-see mental shelf. Corban closed his eyes and tried to clear his mind, but the adrenaline coursing through his veins kept him awake.

He slipped out of the hammock and sat on the floor. Corban lit the lamp and took an old book out of his backpack. Like other sources of information, the book should have been stored in the colony's library ship, but Corban and Thane claimed it as a family heirloom so they weren't required to donate it.

The tattered copy of *Bushcraft: Outdoor Survival Guide* once belonged to their great-grandfather,

Devon Abrams. Corban had read the book from cover to cover several times, memorizing passages about knot-tying and the proper use of a pocketknife. He remained baffled about the chapters on recognizing plants and animals that didn't exist on Vesta, such as poison ivy and rattlesnakes.

Devon had kept a journal on the inside covers and page margins of the handbook. Corban reread the first entry by the dim light.

10-13-V⅄01: The storm took us by surprise, so it was fortunate we hadn't finished stripping the ship's interior. We were able to get inside and seal the airlock before the hurricane hit. We aren't near any large bodies of water, but the storm had all the qualities of a hurricane or typhoon. The powerful winds and torrential rain destroyed almost everything we built or planted over the past six months.

We weren't expecting the storm to last as long as it did and were forced to ration the water. I gave Nia half my portion because she was so dehydrated from the morning sickness. She said she was having second thoughts about having five children, as we agreed to in our settlers' contract. I reminded her the fortress walls would be up by the end of the month, so we'll be safe from future storms and from the monsters—Captain Kaczenski calls the white-haired beasts 'night terrors' because they're terrifying and only come out at night.

The walls of the fort were all that was left standing when we emerged from the ship after the storm. I guess we'll be building everything from stone from now on. There's a family of stonemasons aboard the next scout ship, which should arrive in eighteen months.

Corban was proud of his great-grandparents, but he also questioned their sanity. He was unable to imagine how two people fresh out of college found the courage to join the scouting expedition to Vesta. *Five storms in stasis pods.* He cringed at the thought of being enclosed in a small box for more than five minutes.

For a few of the scouts, the stasis pods became their coffins. The technology was new and untested in Devon and Nia's day. They placed their faith in a vague report from an unmanned probe launched decades before they were born. It was a dangerous one-way trip and the volunteers knew they might not live to see the planet. If they survived the journey, there were no guarantees they would live to establish a settlement.

Of the four hundred and seventy probes launched, fifty-six sent back enough information to justify further investigation with manned scout ships. Of the fifty-six scout teams, seventeen established settlements. Five of the settlements, all named Vesta for reasons Corban couldn't fathom, since each was on a different planet, became successful colonies. Gamma, Epsilon, Zeta, Iota, and Lambda.

One colony was abandoned seventy storms after settlement. Lambda.

Corban shut the book and leaned back against the wall, lost in thought. *Sixteen storms since the last ship. Fifteen storms since the last communication from Earth. They heard the word "plague" and condemned us to exile. They assumed we were all dead, or we'd die soon enough.* Corban didn't blame Earth for refusing to risk any more lives or resources, but to be cut off from their only source of supplies and technology was to betray the thousands who worked hard and sacrificed everything to establish the colony.

His uncle Leighton had been elected mayor of West Fort two storms ago, but the power had gone straight to his head. He had always been a horrible parent, but his violent outbursts escalated after the election. Corban didn't understand why he was the primary target of his uncle's wrath. He needed a way out, and changing guilds was his only logical option. *I need to be brave, like my great-grandparents. But where can I go, and how can I convince Uncle to let me leave?*

He was overcome with a sudden sense of foreboding and got to his feet. "Thane? Wake up!"

"Is the storm over?" Thane shifted in his hammock until he locked eyes with Corban.

An explosion of thunder was followed by a sharp *crack* and a shuddering crash that reverberated through the fortress walls, causing their hammocks to sway.

"Does that answer your question?"

"So some trees are coming down. I'm surprised any trees are left standing on this planet. Did you notice I was trying to sleep through the racket?" Thane yawned.

"I need to talk to you."

"Did you have a premonition?"

Corban hesitated. He needed more time to analyze the strange dream. "Yes and no."

"Was it the one about the weird tree with three trunks?"

"Not this time. This dream was different, but that's not why I woke you."

Thane frowned. "What then?"

Corban climbed back into his hammock. "Is something else going on with Uncle that you're not telling me?"

"What do you mean?"

Corban sensed Thane knew exactly what he meant. "I mean, why the increased hostilities? Have you overheard anything—?"

"You need to keep your mouth shut," Thane said.

Corban was taken aback by the gruff response. "What?"

"I mean you need to keep your mouth shut about your Talent around Uncle. You're not the only Stray he doesn't like."

"But you're a Stray too."

"I think he forgot about my Talent, which is the way it needs to be."

Corban bristled. "I'm not ashamed of my Talent. It's come in handy a few times. Remember, I told him he'd win the election."

"Yes, but my point is you shouldn't mention your dreams around Uncle. They make him nervous."

"Because he can't control them," Corban said bitterly, "like he does with everything else in my life."

"It's more than a control issue, it's fear."

"What have you overheard?" Corban asked.

"It's not just Uncle. The whole council wants to make it illegal for Strays to use their Talents."

"What?" Corban sat up in his hammock but seized the sides before it could flip over. "We can't help having Talents! We didn't ask for them, and we've never hurt anyone! If anything, they've made life easier for the colony as the machines have stopped working!"

"I know, but I'm telling you what I overheard in the council meeting last week. There was a lot of debate about the possibility of Strays using their Talents to manipulate or hurt Survivors. They're scared."

"Darkness! They're stupid! What prompted this? Things were peaceful before Uncle became mayor." When Thane didn't reply, the answer became clear to

Corban. "He campaigned to improve relations between Strays and Survivors. It was all a lie, wasn't it?"

Thane sighed. "I think Leighton's always been paranoid of Strays. He didn't want to raise us."

Corban made an effort to rein in his temper. "He could've turned us over to the orphanage. We would've been better off."

Thane shook his head. "You know there were too many. All the Survivors were expected to take in their relatives' children."

"I wish someone else in the family survived."

"Strays have been saying that for sixteen storms," Thane snapped.

"Sorry." Corban was probing too close to a nerve and needed to be quiet. Thane was old enough to remember the Plague. "You don't have to live here with Uncle anymore. You can move out anytime, you know."

"I'm staying for your sake, until you're old enough to leave."

Corban was stunned by his quiet confession. He had never asked Thane why he didn't move in with the Smiths Guild when he became an adult. Most of them lived in Waterfall, the fortress five kilometers to the south. "You are? I don't know what to say."

"You don't have to say anything. We're brothers. I don't consider Leighton family. He's more like . . . a temporary warden."

"I didn't know."

"For someone who's clairvoyant, you don't seem to notice what's right in front of your face."

Corban bit back a sarcastic response, opting instead for a quiet, "Thank you."

Thane dismissed it with a snort. "Don't wake me again unless the fort's on fire."

THREE
DATAFILES

"What do you think?" Nikki watched her best friend's black, almond-shaped eyes as they skimmed the single sheet of yellowed notebook paper. Every square centimeter of the paper's surface was covered in Nikki's tiny handwriting.

"Maybe you could improve your writing skills if you joined the artists. I hear they have a shortage of poets." Jing Kaczenski laughed and tossed the mid-term essay onto the table between them. "This is mediocre, at best. Are you sure you want to turn it in to Mr. Gupta?"

"I don't have any extra paper, so I can't rewrite it." Nikki poked out her lower lip. Jing was such a perfectionist that Nikki dreaded asking her for help. "Could you fix it, please?"

Jing rolled her eyes. "Pen?"

"It's out of ink." Nikki produced a pencil stub so short, Jing couldn't hold it between her thumb and index finger.

"How am I supposed to make any changes?" Jing looked at the end of the pencil stub and shot Nikki another eye-roll. The eraser was nonexistent.

"Just draw a line through any words and write the changes above them."

"There is no 'above them.'" Jing smoothed out the paper on the tabletop and read aloud. "'The History of Vesta's Stray Population by Nikolasa Macdonald Zegarelli Ramirez'—you could leave off your middle names, that'll save some space—'No one has been able to determine what caused the Plague of twelfth month, VΛ69, which wiped out half of Vesta colony's adult population.' Enthralling opening sentence. I can't wait to see where this leads."

"I don't need the sarcasm," Nikki said. "Help me, please. This is a big grade. Gupta's notorious for piling on assignments after the storm to make up for the missed school days."

"Yes, I've heard he likes to punish students for the weather, as if it's their fault. I'm glad I didn't take his class this semester." Jing squinted to read the next sentence. "'Nor has anyone been able to determine why the Plague spared many children below the age of puberty or why these children, nicknamed Strays, developed Talents as a result.' This is a long, run-on sentence and not much information. Maybe you should see if there's anything about Strays in the datafiles."

Jing reached into the threadbare nylon school bag next to her feet and dug out a blank sheet of paper. "Here—now rewrite the essay so it's legible and less boring." A rare smile split her round face, revealing several dimples and slightly crooked front teeth, which stood out in sharp contrast against her light brown skin and shoulder-length, black bob.

Nikki accepted the gift with a sigh of relief and retrieved her pencil stub. "Thanks—I owe you one."

"I think you own me nine or ten." Jing packed her dog-eared books into her bag. "Sorry I can't help you more with the essay, but I have kitchen duty this afternoon."

"Don't apologize." Nikki sighed again. "I wish there was more to life than schoolwork and domestic drudgery. The only excitement we get around here is the storm."

"If it's excitement you want, you could hunt night terrors."

"You're missing the point, as usual."

"You don't have a point, as usual. See you tomorrow." Jing got to her feet and headed to the main ladder.

Nikki shook her head in mock exasperation and waved at her friend's retreating back. When Jing descended out of sight, Nikki picked up the pencil stub and turned back to her essay.

She's right. These are boring, run-on sentences. Why can't I have a useful Talent, like being able to put words on paper? Nikki got up from the table and crossed the room to one of the six holographic computer stations built into the bulkhead wall. She plopped down in the rickety chair in front of the monitor closest to the left corner, trying to recall if the voice-command still worked on it.

"Search: Stray."

The blue screen faded to a vomit green and didn't respond. *Darkness.* She scooted the chair close enough to touch the screen and tried again, typing *Stray* into the search box.

The screen glowed blue again as it yielded a summary of outdated information.

Stray: the nickname given to Vesta-Lambda colony's prepubescent Plague survivors. It is unclear how they gained their unique mental abilities, but the main theory is epigenetics, or environmental influence. Something in Vesta's environment altered one of their DNA strands to immunize their bodies from the Plague virus. Only children exposed to the virus developed the change in their DNA. It is unclear why colonists above the age of puberty did not develop the same immunity upon exposure.

The altered DNA strand affected a change in the prepubescent brain, giving each Stray an unusual trait commonly referred to as a Talent. [See index 5 for a list of identified Talents.]

With the eradication of the virus due to the discovery of a vaccine by the Herbalists Guild, the DNA alterations ceased. There are approximately 1,017 Strays in Vesta-Lambda colony, or one tenth of the population. [See index 6 for a list of identified Strays.]

The last line made her pause. *There's a list?* Nikki typed *Index 6* into the search box, a knot settling in her stomach as the results filled the screen.

She was on the list, as was Eliana, Derek, and many of her classmates. Nikki couldn't explain why it bothered her.

"Sorry to intrude. I didn't know anyone was up here," a smooth baritone voice announced from behind her.

Nikki stifled a gasp of surprise and twisted around in her chair to see who managed to reach the library level of the ship without her hearing footsteps on the ladder.

A tall young man with athletic shoulders and shoulder-length blond hair, in serious need of scissors, was standing next to the ladder. He wore faded blue jeans, a dark green T-shirt, and bluedeer-leather hiking boots.

His jaw dropped the moment he saw Nikki's face. He stared at her as if he had just seen a ghost.

Nikki resisted the urge to check her hair, knowing no matter how bad it looked, it couldn't be the reason for his reaction. "I guess you're not used to seeing anyone else in the library?"

The young man's stunned expression shifted to an awkward smile. "I don't want to distract you from your research. I'll come back later."

"Do you always make assumptions about people you've just met?"

He shrugged and the smile faded. "I was just being polite."

"It's a long walk or bike ride to get here, no matter which fort you came from." Nikki waved a hand, indicating the five open screens on the wall to her right. "Don't inconvenience yourself on my account. My paper's due tomorrow. I'm sure you're here for the same reason."

"Do you always make assumptions about people you've just met?" His smile appeared genuine. He sauntered across the room, heading for the station one seat over from hers.

Nikki noted the machete tucked into his bluedeer-leather belt. "Hunters Guild?"

He nodded and looked over at her as he took a seat. "I think the voice-command is broken at your station."

"Yes, this one's worthless. I guess you come here often."

"Probably not often enough if you've seen my report card. By the way, I'm Corban Abrams, West Fort."

"Nikki Ramirez, Lakeside."

"Which guild?"

His eyes were brown, although his lashes and eyebrows were blond like his hair. It was an unusual combination, but she thought it suited him. "It's complicated."

Corban grinned. "How?"

"My parents were farmers, but my mother wanted to focus on herbs and changed guilds. She's a partner in the Herbalists Guild, but she's also a nurse in the Medics Guild." She shifted her gaze to her screen. "My father's still with the farmers."

"So are you a medic, farmer, or herbalist?" Corban's voice dropped to a whisper. "Sorry about your parents, but at least they survived the Plague— mine didn't."

"Sorry about your parents," Nikki echoed with a pang of sympathy. "I'd like to be a medic, but my Talent—" she hesitated, unsure of how much to disclose. "Let's say it's incompatible with that career path. I'm an apprentice herbalist."

"Your Talent is incompatible with medicine?" He looked confused but didn't press for an explanation. "I'd like to learn more about the Medics Guild."

Her eyebrows shot up in surprise. She was unable to tell from his tone if he was teasing or serious. "Is that your homework assignment?"

Corban laughed again. "Researching another guild? No, today I need to write a report for biology. I have to describe the properties of Zegarellium."

Nikki drew in a sharp breath before she could stop herself.

Apparently Corban didn't consider staring bad manners as he turned to her again. "Something wrong?"

She tried to cover the gaffe. "No, it's because I'm . . . familiar with that particular herb."

"Everyone's heard of Zegarellium." He appraised her expression with a suspicious frown. "It cured the Plague. Without it, everyone over the age of twelve would've died. Are you saying you know more than what's in the datafiles?"

"A little bit, yes. I've . . . met the herbalist who discovered it."

"You've *met* her?" The awkward silence stretched for a minute as Corban turned to his screen and made a request. "Search: Discovery of Zegarellium."

Nikki's face grew warmer as she turned to stare at her own monitor again.

"It says here Solona Zegarelli has two daughters, Eliana Ramirez, born in 62, and Nikolasa Ramirez, born in 69. That would make . . . Nikki . . . about seventeen storms."

From the corner of her eye, Nikki saw him studying her, one eyebrow arched. He looked more amused than anything other emotion she could identify, but she stared straight ahead at her screen to avert her red face. "What the file won't tell you is Mom found the cure by accident. She was weeding a patch of sage when she dug up the root of a—"

"Zegarellium," Corban supplied.

"—Mom hadn't seen it before, so she added it to the pile of native plants for testing. The medics were getting desperate—"

"Darkness. Everyone was desperate," Corban interrupted again, although she didn't think he meant to be rude. "People were dying in less than forty-eight hours. It swept through the colony like a wildfire."

Nikki nodded. "The medics tested the native herbs on themselves as fast as they could process them. Mom's discovery happened to be the right one. They were able to vaccinate everyone twelve and older. Even people who caught the Plague recovered if they got the Zegarellium in time."

"Native virus cured by a native plant." His tone held newfound respect. "Your mother's a hero."

"I hope it helps a little with your report." Nikki was eager to change the subject. She hated living in the shadow of her famous mother. "Now that you know something about me, why don't you tell me something about yourself? How old are you?"

He smiled. A small corner was chipped off one of his otherwise-perfect front teeth. "How old do I look?"

From his jovial manner, she guessed young. "Fifteen?"

"Seventeen."

"I guess we were both infants during the Plague." Nikki blew out a long breath. "I'm glad I was too young to remember."

"My brother Thane was three. He remembers but refuses to talk about it."

"My sister's the same way. What's your Talent, if you don't mind me asking?"

"Clairvoyance." Corban leaned his chair back on two legs. "My uncle thinks it's useless."

It was Nikki's turn to be impressed. "Can you really see the future?"

"Sometimes." He studied her face for a moment, as if he wanted to say more, but then shook his head and looked away. "It's complicated, and I still don't understand how to use it because the visions come to me in dreams. I also have the issue of being empathic."

"I've never heard of anyone with two Talents. What does empathic mean?"

"It means I can sense emotions."

Nikki felt a flutter of concern. "You can . . . read minds?"

Corban shook his head. "I don't know what people are thinking, but I can sense what they're feeling."

Nikki bit her lip. "Isn't it the same thing?"

"No." He frowned. "It's more like having a built-in lie detector. For example, I knew you were holding something back about Zegarellium."

"It wouldn't be because I'm a terrible actress?" Nikki forced a smile. "Can you sense anything else about me?"

His eyebrow went up again. "I can sense I make you nervous."

She was sure he guessed that from her flaming-red face. "If you're that perceptive, your uncle doesn't know what he's talking about. You have a useful Talent."

A dark cloud crossed Corban's features when she mentioned his uncle, but then it was gone. "What's your Talent that's incompatible with medicine?"

"Actually, I'm not supposed to talk about it— Mom's orders."

"So both our families are ashamed of our Talents?"

Nikki bristled. "She's not ashamed—"

Corban interrupted before she could start an argument. "I shouldn't have said that since I don't even know you. Thane says I'm tactless." He appraised her expression again. "I sense you'd agree with him."

She reined in her defensive reaction but was determined to change the subject before he asked for more details. "I really have to write this paper and get back to Lakeside before dark."

Corban looked disappointed for a fleeting moment, but then he smiled. "Me too." He appeared reluctant to turn to his screen. "Thanks for the info on Zegarellium. It'll be nice to get a good grade for a change."

"You're welcome." She faced her own screen.

The sudden silence was awkward, but Nikki was determined not to embarrass herself again by striking up a new conversation. She stared at the blue-green haze for ten minutes without reading any of the information. She couldn't concentrate with Corban sitting so close and mustered all her self-control to keep her eyes on the screen. Knowing he sensed her embarrassment made the atmosphere doubly awkward.

Knowing he probably sensed that she found him attractive made her want to crawl under a chair and hide.

Nikki didn't have many friends—and preferred it that way—but something about Corban Abrams made her wish for a little more experience socializing with members of the opposite sex. She pretended to jot down a few notes before collecting her backpack and slipping off to the ladder.

"Can I see you again?" Corban called after her before she began her descent.

She missed a rung and scrambled to find a foothold so she wouldn't fall. "You want to see me again?"

"Yes." She detected amusement in his tone. He turned around in his chair to look at her, but since he wasn't laughing, she was hopeful he hadn't noticed her clumsy display.

She didn't know what to say to his request and blurted out the first thing that popped into her head. "I have an Earth history paper due next week. I'll be back here seventh-day morning to do the research."

He turned back to his screen before she glimpsed his expression. "Maybe I'll see you then."

Maybe I need a lesson on how not to act like a moron in front of an attractive guy, Nikki thought as she descended to the airlock.

FOUR
CACHE

Corban sat alone in the library ship for an hour, but he couldn't concentrate on the screen. He reread the same paragraph four times, but none of the information was registering. His mind had been in turmoil since the moment he saw Nikki Ramirez's face.

The girl from my dream! The same enraged female who would attempt to decapitate Corban with his uncle's sword—and probably succeed. He couldn't believe it. *I met my own murderer and tried to ask her out! Darkness. Am I crazy?*

He imagined Thane's advice. *"Why do you want to see her again if you already know she's going to kill you? Are you insane?"*

But the mystery of Nikki Ramirez was too compelling. Corban rationalized that he needed to know more about her to understand the premonition. Maybe he could do something to alter his fate. His dreams always turned out exactly the way he saw them, but this one needed to be an exception. *I have to change the outcome. My life depends on it!*

37

He gave up the attempt to write his biology paper, resigned himself to another F in the class, and climbed the ladder down to the airlock. Corban grimaced when he stepped outside. Ilios was lower in the sky than he anticipated. He needed to move fast to make it back to West Fort before the gates were closed for the night.

He checked to see if his multi-tool utility knife was in his back pocket. Corban found the tiny pen light attachment and clicked it on to make sure the solar battery had some life left. It gave off a feeble glow, but it would help cut the inky darkness of the woods, if needed.

Corban hoped he didn't need it. He wasted a valuable minute debating whether he should spend the night in the library but talked himself out of the idea. He couldn't afford another tardy in his first class, which he was already in danger of failing. Besides, his brother would worry, and Corban didn't want Thane risking his life again searching for him after dark.

Guilt was strong motivation to get moving. He descended the gangway and sprinted across the weed-choked tarmac to the wide bridge. The dirt path divided on the opposite side of the bridge. The right fork followed the shoreline to Lakeside; the left fork cut through the forest to West Fort.

Corban ran flat out for two kilometers before a shin splint forced him to stop, stretch, and catch his breath. It took him five breaths to realize he had chosen the worst possible place to stop.

He tensed, glancing around at the thick hardwood trees on either side of the path. Something rustled in the undergrowth to his left, something that gave off a rank odor of rotten meat.

Night terror? Corban silently drew his machete and backed away from the shrubbery. *But night terrors make so much noise, and they never come out in the daytime. What else could it be?*

He kept moving away from the rustling, not taking his eyes off the bushes in case the night terror, or whatever it was, attacked. He was ten paces away and thinking of making a run for it when he saw a flash of blue between the bright green leaves.

Bluedeer! Corban was relieved he decided not to run. Though bluedeer weren't as dangerous as night terrors, they were a threat to the unwary and pursued anything that moved. It was safer to stand still and wait for it to lose interest.

Long-legged reptilian creatures, bluedeer were more like the crocodiles Corban had studied in database holograms than the white-tail deer his great-grandfather Devon once hunted on Earth. Corban should have been able to see the head above the bushes. *Why does it stink like a night terror?*

He didn't move for five minutes, waiting to see if the bluedeer showed itself. The rustling continued. Curiosity piqued, he gathered his courage and moved quietly up to the shrubbery.

Raising the machete high above his head, Corban brought it down on the bush with all his strength, snapping tender branches and connecting with something solid. It emitted a shriek of surprise and hit the ground with a *thud.*

He raised the machete, ready to strike again if the first blow didn't incapacitate the beast, but he detected no sound or movement from the underbrush. He waited, making himself to count to ten before probing the bushes with the tip of his machete. Meeting no resistance, he parted the branches.

It was a half-grown bluedeer, too small to turn over to the Tanners Guild for one pair of boots. His machete left a deep, bloody indentation in the top of its ugly skull. The yellow eyes bulged and the green tongue lolled on the ground between exposed saw-like teeth.

Corban held his nose against the stench as he shoved the carcass aside with his foot. Bluedeer were scavengers and he was curious to see what this one uncovered.

The grisly remains of a night terror were beneath the body. That explained the familiar stench but brought up a new question. *What killed the night terror?* The vicious, white-furred beasts resembled Earth polar bears, except they hunted in packs like wolves. "Land sharks" were how Devon Abrams described them in his journal. Night terrors were at the top of the Vesta food chain—nothing hunted them. The colonists only killed them in self-defense because the predators tasted as bad as they smelled.

Holding his breath, Corban squatted down and examined what was left of the night terror carcass. He was shocked to discover a bullet hole in the skull, near the right eye socket.

Few colonists still owned firearms. With a depleted supply of ammunition for rifles, the Hunters Guild switched to machetes a few storms back. Some of the old-timers owned bows, but the rest of the guild improvised with traps, slings, and anything else they were able to make by hand.

Corban straightened up, tucked his machete back into his belt, and noted the lengthening shadows with concern. Before he turned back to the path, something else caught his eye. He stared at the woods past the dead animals as the familiar chill of déjà vu washed over him.

Rising out of the shrubbery a few meters in front of him was a large hardwood tree with three trunks, each as big around as his entire body. Corban had seen this strange sight before, in one of his dreams.

It's late. I need to get home before dark. But curiosity muscled aside common sense, and he walked around the carcasses to reach the tree.

Corban ran a hand over the smooth black bark. Nothing was unusual about the tree that he could see in the fading light. He walked around it, gazing up at the canopy of branches. It was the same tree from his dream.

Why am I here? What's special about this tree? Why did I see it in a premonition?

He knew the wise thing to do was come back when it was daylight to investigate, but he couldn't ignore his burning curiosity.

Corban kept walking. He was three-quarters of the way around the trunks when he stepped on something that wasn't dirt. His heart raced as he brought his heel down a few times, testing the strange spot. It sounded like wood, with a hollow space beneath it.

Despite the warning in his mind to get home, Corban stooped down and ran his hands over the rough wooden panel, which was about two meters square. It was half-hidden by dirt and weeds, but he wasted no time finding an edge to raise it.

The wood was heavy, and he was nervous about what he might find under it. He lifted the panel half a meter, got down on one knee, and balanced the edge against his leg. He pulled out the utility knife with the pen light and shone the narrow beam down into the hole.

A gleam of metal caught his eye. Corban's apprehension turned to confusion as he played the tiny light around.

A large pile of rifles filled the dug-out shallow space. The entire cache was wrapped in a layer of clear plastic. He estimated one hundred rifles with ten to twelve pistols tossed into the mix. *I didn't think there were this many weapons in the entire colony.*

Corban rose to his feet and dropped the heavy panel back into place. He brushed the dirt from his hands, thinking. It was tempting to take one of the pistols, but he had an uneasy feeling it would be missed. Someone had gone to a great deal of trouble to collect and hide these guns, but who and why?

He kicked dirt back over the panel, concealing the edges as he had found it. His mind churned with questions, but there was no time left for thinking as the last remnants of Ilios disappeared.

The immediate absence of daylight brought the blood-curdling growls of night terrors, echoing through the woods. Corban figured he had five minutes or less to find shelter. He stared up at the dark canopy of the strange tree and decided to go vertical.

Without proper equipment, it was difficult to climb Vesta's slick-barked hardwood trees, but the trunks of the premonition tree grew close enough together that Corban used it to his advantage. Bracing his hands and feet against opposing trunks, he was able to ascend to the lowest branches, twenty meters off the ground.

He managed to straddle a thick branch just as a pack of night terrors surrounded the base of the tree, their white coats visible in the reflected light of Vesta's stars. Corban wrapped his arms around the nearest trunk and tried to recall everything he knew about the predators. One crucial fact eluded him. *Can they climb trees?*

His heart pounded as he watched the night terrors circle the tree, snarling and barking up at him, their fanged muzzles dripping with saliva. The stench of decay was so bad, it made his eyes water. It was a mystery how the filthy beasts kept their fur white. They stood on hind legs and clawed at the bark, stripping chunks off the tree, but remained on the ground, to his relief.

Nocturnal insects buzzed around Corban's face and he swatted them away with impatience. The white-tailed gnats and lightning flies preferred to feast on the blood of native animals, but that didn't prevent them from being a nuisance. He waved a swarm away from his left ear, wishing he had the foresight to put a hooded jacket in his backpack.

Some of the night terrors lost interest in him and went over to the bluedeer carcass. While the monsters made short work of Corban's kill, he took advantage of the brief respite to figure out how to contact Thane. His brother knew he had gone to the library ship, and would probably ask the sentries if Corban returned to the fort before the gates closed.

He shook his head, wondering what he would do if their situations were reversed. Would he search for Thane outside the fort after dark? Corban broke out in a cold sweat as he thought back to the night eight storms ago when Thane almost lost his leg—and his life.

No matter how hard he tried, he couldn't remember why he was outside the gates alone when darkness fell. Vesta toddlers knew better, so how did Corban, as a boy of nine, end up in such a predicament? He had asked Thane about it a few times, but his brother's recollection was hazy too. "I heard you call for help and somehow got past the closed gates. It all happened so fast," was the longest explanation Thane had given him. "I found you before the night terror attacked and tried to protect you from it."

Corban recalled a few members of the Hunters Guild driving off the beast with their rifles. The men rushed the boys inside the gates before the night terror returned with reinforcements from its pack. Thane spent a week in the fort's infirmary and another week in the hospital ship where Medics Guild surgeons salvaged what remained of his leg. A month of physical therapy followed before Thane was able to walk again. Corban could never make up for what happened, but Thane never blamed him.

Although they were older and hopefully wiser now, Corban knew he wouldn't hesitate to go after Thane if he wound up outside the fort after dark.

Thane's Talent was the obvious answer to his dilemma. Corban didn't know the extent of his brother's hearing range. *How far am I from the fort? Two kilometers?*

It was worth a try. "Thane!" Corban shouted, "Thane Abrams! It's Corban! I'm safe! Don't leave the fort! I'm safe!"

"Corban is safe! Don't leave the fort!" He kept it up for a long time, shouting until he was hoarse.

Meanwhile, the night terrors kept vigil at the base of the tree, growling and rising on hind legs to claw at the bark. Corban resigned himself to a sleepless night but knew it could have been worse. He hoped they caught the scent of something else and left him alone.

After a few hours, a portion of the pack raced off into the woods in pursuit of something, but the same hunters dragged two bluedeer carcasses back to Corban's tree for the rest of the pack to enjoy.

Corban grimaced at the bloody feast going on below. He regretted not taking one of the guns from the cache for extra protection.

I really should think things through better—like asking out girls who'll probably murder me. He yawned and shifted his position on the branch to restore the circulation to his limbs. All he could do was stay awake and wait for Ilios to rise.

FIVE
STONE WALLS

Thane lay awake in his hammock, focusing his Talent on the distant shouts of his idiot brother. "Corban is safe! Don't leave the fort!"

Darkness. He doesn't sound safe. The growling and snarls from the night terrors in the same location continued unabated, but since Corban kept up the caterwauling, Thane assumed he took shelter up a tree. Safe for the moment, but he would be stranded all night. *Why didn't he leave the library before it got dark? After that premonition about some girl cutting off his head in the peach orchard, you'd think he'd be more concerned about his own safety.* Thane hoped Corban remembered the dream wrong. Perhaps it was a real nightmare and not a premonition.

Thane had become more protective of Corban as their uncle had become more abusive. Although Thane weathered his share of verbal abuse, Leighton held a grudge against Corban that defied explanation. The mayor seemed determined to take out all his frustrations on the younger brother. *If I had both my legs, I'd teach Uncle a lesson.*

He snorted, ashamed of himself for the cowardly excuse. Thane wanted to stand up to their uncle once and for all, but he needed to be patient and wait until Corban had somewhere else to go. Living space was at a premium on Vesta. People lived with their families or their guilds, period. The waiting list for apartments was lengthy, and Strays always went to the bottom of the list. Thane figured he didn't need to think about getting married until he was thirty.

If any woman will have me. He shifted his ruined leg to a more comfortable position in the hammock.

His own standing in the Smiths Guild was tenuous. As a Stray, he was used to being treated as an inferior, but his supervisor had yet to offer him a regular position in the guild. This meant Thane would have no place to live if he moved out of his uncle's apartment. At twenty storms, he was still an apprentice when he should have moved up to assistant by now.

He yawned, desperate for sleep, yet he needed to keep an ear on Corban. He resigned himself to a sleepless night, dozing off when he heard his brother open the door to their room shortly after dawn.

***

Thane awoke mid-afternoon, his first cognizant thought—*I'm in trouble.* Corban was still asleep in the other hammock so he quietly got dressed and strapped on his leg brace. He made his way as fast as his bad leg allowed to the metal-smith shed in the marketplace.

Chaim Rajamani was Smiths Guild master, in charge of all the ironware produced in the colony.

The forge supervisors at the other five forts reported to him. He was a bald, widowed, humorless man in his mid-forties. Since he lived in West Fort, he was often at the shed, supervising the four apprentice metal-smiths, and he made it no secret Thane was his least favorite.

Thane found him at his own workstation.

"This better be good, Abrams!" Chaim's bellow was louder than the pounding of hammers on anvils at the other three stations.

Knowing his excuse had to sound convincing, Thane said, "Food poisoning. I was up vomiting most of the night." Food poisoning wasn't an uncommon occurrence in the colony when apprentice cooks didn't have enough supervision.

"I didn't hear about anyone else getting sick." Chaim eyed him with mistrust. The feeling was mutual.

"Sorry, I came as soon as I felt well enough to leave the apartment. I'll take over what you're working on." He reached out to take the hammer from Chaim, but the guild master waved him away.

"The day's almost over and, thanks to you, I didn't have time to deliver your uncle's order of hinges to the construction site. So you're going to take them."

"Will I be able to get back before dark?"

"That's your problem." Chaim shoved the tongs into the coals, turning his back on Thane. "I suggest you get moving."

"Yes, sir."

Thane turned to leave, but Chaim barked at him over his shoulder, "Miss another day of work for anything but the storm and you're out of the guild!"

"Yes, sir." Thane felt as if he had been punched him in the stomach. He made his way to the small

48

marketplace parking lot where a single Smiths Guild delivery truck sat rusting, its black paint peeling and faded to a mottled gray. The contents in the truck bed were covered with a tarp, and the tiny cab was open to the elements with a half-windshield to discourage insects from pelting the driver.

Thane slid into the driver's seat and touched the ignition button. The electric truck rumbled to life, although the aging engine wheezed and sputtered as if it intended to die at any moment. He put it in gear and headed down the cobbled streets to the main gates.

Once outside West Fort, he took the gravel road south toward Waterfall. No shock absorbers were left in the truck, so it was a rough ride and slow going. It took him an hour to cover the five kilometers to the fork in the road near the bridge to Waterfall. Here he took the right fork, turning away from Waterfall and continuing the uncomfortable drive toward Orchard Valley.

After two kilometers, the woods gave way to pastures. He cast an uneasy glance at the orchards in the lower valley as he took the left fork when the road divided again. He eased the truck onto a new road made up of muddy ruts with no trace of gravel. Thane's back ached from all the bouncing as he drove the last three kilometers to the construction site of the new fort, near the banks of the Cold River. The entire drive had taken him two hours.

Confusion and anxiety washed over him in equal measures as he noted the three-story stone walls. As far as Thane knew, construction wasn't scheduled until the next storm, yet the exterior of the fort appeared to be finished. Large stacks of lumber, doors, and crates of windows were piled near the main gates. Thane parked the truck next to a blue flatbed with *Glaziers Guild* painted on the driver's side door in faded white letters. He cut the engine and his uncle emerged from the gates.

"You're late!" Leighton snapped before Thane climbed from the cab. "Where's Chaim?"

"He asked me to drive." Thane's left leg ached from the jarring ride. He took his time getting to his feet before facing his uncle. His gaze swept the building supplies but he knew better than to ask.

"I told that idiot not to send a worthless Stray to do his job!"

From a lifetime of self-mastery, Thane didn't react. "I'll help you unload. Where do you want the hinges?"

"Unload it yourself! This should've been here five hours ago, and I'm busy!" Leighton pointed to an open spot between the piles of supplies, fifteen meters from where Thane parked. "Put it over there, and make sure you don't damage anything!"

"Yes, sir." Thane didn't see a way to maneuver the truck any closer to the spot indicated. He moved to the tailgate and removed the tarp. His left leg gave a stab of pain, protesting the weight of the first wooden box he lifted from the truck bed. The crate was filled to the brim with iron hinges. Out of the corner of his eye, Thane noted Leighton's malicious grin, but he kept his mouth shut.

"One more thing," Leighton said before stalking back inside the gates, "you tell anyone about this and I'll give Corban a leg to match yours. Do I make myself clear?"

"Yes, sir." Thane pressed his lips together, not trusting himself to hold back what he wanted to say.

There weren't enough foul words in his vocabulary to describe his uncle.

His arms and back managed the heavy boxes with no problem, but his bad leg was unaccustomed to supporting so much weight. He looked around but saw no sign of a hand truck or a construction worker to lend assistance. He had no choice but to manage the task on his own. Thane limped his way back and forth across the muddy ground, carrying the boxes one at a time. His leg was throbbing by the time he lifted the eighth and last box from the truck bed.

Thane confirmed Ilios's position in the sky after he set down the final box and hobbled back to the truck. The vehicle needed to be returned to the fleet warehouse at Waterfall, and then he had to find a way back to West Fort before dark.

He heard his uncle dismissing the construction workers for the day. *Who'd be crazy enough to put a hunter in charge of constructing a fort?*

Unless no one did. Thane slid into the driver's seat and started the ignition. *He appointed himself supervisor.* As he headed north toward Waterfall, he stared at the fort in the rearview mirror. *Trusting him to build a fort is crazy. He already made a huge mistake.*

The stone walls had no openings for windows.

Ignoring his aching leg and the complaints from the engine on life support, Thane pushed the accelerator hard, grateful he only needed his right leg to drive. He didn't have much time to make it to Waterfall before dark.

Twice the size of the other forts, Waterfall had been built on a high plateau overlooking Cold River's natural fifty-meter plunge. A hydroelectric dam harnessed the power of the river, providing the

51

colony with electricity for the dwindling fleet of ground transportation.

It was nearing dusk when Thane drove across the dam. He maneuvered the truck through the fort's open gates and pulled in behind a line of battered vehicles on the ramp leading underground to the fleet warehouse. Reaching the basement parking deck, he was directed to a free space. A Mechanics Guild apprentice connected the engine to a recharging station before Thane climbed from the cab.

"Thanks." He nodded to the young woman, who was already moving over to plug in the next vehicle.

Now what? Thane followed the crowd of drivers moving toward the stairs. "What's for dinner?" was the main topic of conversation. No one gave him a second glance unless they noticed his brace. The curious stares didn't bother him like they used to, when he was younger.

He emerged from the stairwell at the street level and frowned up at the sky. It was dusk.

"Hey, Stumpy, what're you doing in Waterfall?"

Thane turned to face Rupert Conquist, his best friend in the guild. "I should ask you the same thing, Rhubarb." He shook hands with a young man in sweat-stained coveralls. Rupert was a sight with his mop of flame-red hair, Ilios-burned cheeks, and goofy, lopsided grin. "Chaim send you on an errand, too?"

"The slime worm had me splitting wood all day near Lakeside. I just returned the truck."

"Me too, but I've got to get back to West Fort tonight."

Rupert peered at the sky as they fell into step with the crowd heading to the dining hall. "There's no way. The gates close in maybe fifteen minutes."

"Let me borrow your bike."

His friend eyed his brace. "You have a Talent I don't know about?"

"No, but I have a brother who'll probably search for me if I don't turn up before dark."

"Want me to send him a message?"

"I thought your range was limited." Thane had received mental messages from Rupert before, but only when they were both inside West Fort.

"I've been practicing, sending poetry to Yasmin Wang every night since the storm, trying to convince her to attend the guild formal with me."

Thane squinted into Rupert's face to see if he was joking. He wasn't. "Where does Yasmin live?"

"East Fort."

"And she can hear you from West Fort?"

Rupert shrugged. "I think so. She smiled at me and didn't threaten to put a tourniquet around my neck when I saw her yesterday."

"Maybe she didn't have a tourniquet with her." Thane sighed. What choice did he have? "Give it a try. Tell Corban I'm spending the night in Waterfall."

"That's it?" Rupert scoffed.

"That's it. No poetry, please."

His friend screwed his eyes shut for a moment. "There, done. Now let's get some food. I'm starving."

The dining hall buffet table was filled with platters of baked fish, steamed vegetables, assorted salads, and no bread or desserts. Thane wasn't impressed by the healthy selection, but he followed Rupert's lead, filling his plate with some of everything. They found a table with two empty chairs and made short work of their meal. It was the first time Thane had eaten all day and he was too hungry to interrupt his chewing with small talk.

They deposited their empty plates at the dishwasher's alcove and made their way to the Smiths Guild's barracks on the second floor northeast corner apartment.

"Hey, Rupert!" Several of the other metal-smith assistants greeted Thane's friend as they walked into the large room filled with bunk beds and foot lockers, arranged like a military barracks. A few nodded to Thane, but most of them gawked at his leg and turned away.

Thane kept his face blank. He knew he was considered too weak to do the work of a smith, but he had demonstrated his worth every day for the past two storms and was determined not to let the snubbing get to him.

"When do you officially move in here?" he asked Rupert when they entered a small adjoining room where three derelict couches were pushed up against the walls. The remaining wall contained a widescreen holo-vid projector which stopped working five storms ago.

"Next week." Rupert shrugged.

Thane sat on one couch, testing to see if it had any springs left. It didn't. "I'm glad Chaim promoted you. You deserve it."

Rupert flopped next to him and unlaced his boots. "You deserve it more. You're a better smith than I am. Chaim's a bigot."

"He knows you're a Stray?"

"He's never mentioned it. He probably assumes I'm Normal." Rupert looked embarrassed. "I'm sorry he's such a slime worm."

Thane shrugged, rubbing his aching leg. He peered through the doorway to make sure the other smiths were out of hearing range before lowering his voice to a whisper. "Do you know about Seventh Fort?"

"The one your uncle's proposed?" Rupert asked.

"The one that's almost finished," Thane said.

Rupert looked askance at him. "What?"

"The walls are up."

"No wonder they wanted all those hinges finished." Rupert moved to another couch and stretched out. "Why isn't this common knowledge? Do you know what the mayor's up to?"

Thane frowned. "No, but I intend to find out."

SIX
SUSPICIONS

Corban was getting dressed when Thane walked into their room a few minutes after dawn.

"Don't ever hitch a ride on a bike with Rhubarb," Thane said in lieu of a greeting. He rubbed his aching backside for emphasis.

"So Rupert can send thoughts to people's minds? When did he figure that out?" Corban pulled on his right boot.

"He's always been able to send messages. He wasn't sure how far they'd reach." Thane went to his dresser for clean clothes. "We didn't know if you got the message."

"Obviously, I did. He said, 'Hey, stupid, your brother's spending the night in Waterfall so don't feed yourself to the night terrors.'"

Thane snorted. "Eloquent, as always. Hey, wait for me and let's get breakfast."

"I'll be late for school," Corban said without conviction.

Thane shrugged. "You're always late."

"I missed yesterday. If I miss another day, I'm going to fail most of my classes."

"Yesterday wasn't fun for me, either. Chaim said if I miss another day of work, he'll kick me out of the guild."

"What!" Corban laced up his left boot. "He can't do that! This is only—what?—the third or fourth time you've missed in two storms?"

Thane shook his head. "Forget it. I'll tell you about my day later. First, I need a shower and some food."

Fifteen minutes later, they were ready to head to the dining hall.

Corban asked, "What does Chaim think he'll accomplish by kicking you out of the guild?"

Thane pulled the door shut, and they went downstairs to the street. "I said forget it. Let's talk about something else, like your little adventure in the woods, night before last."

"Let's find a table first." Corban led the way into the dining hall. He took a plate from the stack and perused the buffet table where platters of baked goods, scrambled eggs, sausages, and sliced fresh fruit were set out by members of the Cooks Guild.

"Eggs look edible." Thane selected a plate and filled it with some of everything before heading to a table in the far corner of the crowded dining area. "Our food's better than Waterfall's. They must have a nutritionist on staff. It's all healthy and disgusting."

Corban joined him with a plate piled high with rolls and sausages. "We have better cooks, but the next time I have kitchen duty, I refuse to gut fish."

"You don't have a choice in what chores you're given," Thane said around a mouthful of eggs. "You don't want Ms. Piroux waving a cleaver at you, shouting, 'You don't work, you don't eat.'"

Corban looked toward the kitchen to make sure the Cooks Guild master, Gina Piroux, was out of hearing range. "I'm tired of fish." He bit into a roll, pretended to choke, and poured himself a cup of water from the pitcher at their table, gulping it down like a dying man.

"Now, about your night in the woods . . ." Thane didn't seem to be in the mood for Corban's comic routine.

"Remember my premonition about the tree with three trunks?"

Thane dropped his fork. "You saw it?"

"I found it by accident," Corban said. "I stopped to rest and there it was."

"Rest?" Thane retrieved the fork from his lap. "You were running? Why?"

"Because it was getting dark, moron."

"I'm not the moron who was outside the fort after dark."

Corban rolled his eyes. "Do you want to hear the story or not?"

Thane listened without comment as Corban explained how he was delayed by the bluedeer, discovered the night terror carcass, and noticed the tree.

"I walked around it and found a wooden panel on the ground." He lowered his voice to a whisper. "It was covering a hole filled with guns."

Thane dropped his roll. "Guns?"

"Wrapped in plastic. Lots of them."

"Why would someone hide a cache of weapons?"

Corban stared him down. "You tell me."

Thane frowned. "Uncle."

Corban's eyes widened. "You're sure?"

"No, but I know he's up to something. Yesterday I drove a delivery truck to the seventh fort site, and guess what? The exterior's finished, and Uncle's been supervising the construction."

"What!" It came out louder than Corban intended.

"Shhhh!" Thane glanced around at the other diners. "Keep it down. Uncle said he'd give you a leg to match mine if I told anyone."

"He said that?" Muttering obscenities under his breath, Corban pushed his plate away. "What should we do?"

"Nothing, for now. I think we know too much already. I'm sure Uncle's going to keep an eye on me now that I know about the fort. We can't let him know we found the guns. Just keep your mouth shut, and don't go back to the tree."

"Do you think someone will notice the cache was disturbed?"

"You didn't take anything out of it? Did you put it back the way you found it?"

Corban nodded. "But I'll bet some dirt fell down onto the plastic when I raised the panel."

Thane speared a last bite of eggs with his fork. "I'm sure some dirt normally drifts down into the hole."

"I don't know. It looked clean."

"Even if it looks like it was disturbed, no one will know you were the one who found it."

Corban reached for his abandoned plate, retrieving a half-eaten sausage. "I wish I had your optimism."

They were quiet for a few minutes, lost in thought.

"So why did you stay so late at the library?" Thane shoved a last bite of roll into his mouth.

Corban took his time clearing his throat before replying. "I met . . . a girl."

Thane laughed, clapping a hand over his mouth so he wouldn't spray crumbs on the table. "You didn't get any studying done?"

"It's not like that." Corban rolled his eyes again. "Nothing happened."

"Nothing?" Thane smirked.

"We talked for a few minutes then she took off like I had the Plague."

"You must've made quite an impression. What's her name?"

"Nikki Ramirez." Corban answered the follow-up questions before Thane asked them. "Lakeside. Herbalists Guild. Stray."

"Pretty?"

"Yes." Corban broke eye contact, embarrassed by the detour the conversation had taken.

"Are you going to see her again?"

"Yes, seventh-day morning. She has to write a research paper."

"Is she going to tutor you? Didn't you need help with—what was the class?—anatomy?"

Corban kicked Thane's good leg under the table. "Sorry I mentioned it. Why don't we talk about your love life instead?"

Thane's smile vanished. "Let's not."

"Weren't you going to ask Anika to the guild formal?"

"I was thinking of asking someone less shallow."

"You mean someone less annoying?"

Thane dropped his fork onto his empty plate. "Let's not talk about women anymore. Why don't you have some fruit? It's a wonder you don't have a vitamin deficiency."

Corban shoved the last bite of sausage into his mouth. "Yes, Mother."

SEVEN
OVERHEARD

Nikki paused outside the Kaczenski apartment, fist frozen in midair as she was about to knock, but changed her mind when she heard raised male voices. She didn't intend to eavesdrop but it was impossible not to hear every word.

"There's nothing wrong with me, *Baba*!" Jing's older brother Zhao was shouting.

Their father Kun matched his volume, but his words were in a language Nikki didn't understand. She suspected it was Mandarin, their ancient ancestral language Jing showed no interest in learning. Nikki guessed whatever Kun was shouting was profanity, based on Zhao's reaction.

"What did you call me? I'm your son, not some criminal!"

Kun's Mandarin rebuttal was short and harsh.

"I can't help having a Talent! Would you rather I died in the Plague, like *Ma*? What about Jing?" Zhao went on without waiting for a response from his father. "*Ma* received the vaccine too late. I know you miss her, but aren't you grateful your children survived? The Plague altered my DNA, just as it did for many other children. We can't change what happened. Why are you so afraid of Strays?"

Nikki listened hard, hoping Kun's answer was in Common since she was eager to know the reason herself. *Yes, why are you afraid of your own son?*

She was disappointed the response was in Mandarin, but at least it succeeded in lowering the volume on Zhao's next words.

"I told you I can't move into the Mechanics Guild until I pass my apprenticeship test next month. I have nowhere else to go, *Baba*. You'd send me outside the fort like a criminal?"

Kun's answer was a single word. Nikki guessed it was an affirmative because the next voice she heard was Jing's.

"No! If Zhao goes, I go!"

"Be quiet, *mei mei*!" Kun shouted. "You don't know what you're talking about!"

"I mean it, *Baba*." Jing lowered the volume a fraction. "If you make Zhao leave now, I'll leave too. And I'll never come back to this house."

Nikki decided this would be an opportune time to rescue Jing. She knocked softly, but it sounded like a gunshot because the three Kaczenskis chose that moment to fall silent.

"Darkness! Who is that at this hour?" Kun said.

"It's for me." Jing opened the door a crack and peered out at Nikki.

"Is this a bad time?" Nikki eyed Jing's nightgown.

Jing grimaced, glancing back over her shoulder at her father and brother, who were glaring daggers at each other from opposite sides of the kitchen. "I forgot you were coming over. I'll be right out." She shut the door, leaving Nikki alone in the hallway.

She emerged two minutes later, dressed and carrying her school bag. She slammed the door shut behind her. A single tear made its way down the side of Jing's nose, but she wiped it away with the cuff of her sleeve. The two young women made their way downstairs to the street.

"Want to tell me what's going on?" Nikki said after they passed the gates to exit Lakeside. "I heard shouting."

"Not right now." Jing sniffled. "Want to tell me why you don't want to go to the library ship by yourself?"

Nikki didn't make eye contact. "I'm meeting someone . . . a boy."

Jing's mood improved. "Is he bringing a friend?"

"No, sorry. This isn't a date."

"So you need me to chaperone?" Jing smirked.

Nikki shrugged. "I'm just nervous. You know I turn into a babbling idiot around boys. I'm not sure if he likes me or he thinks I'm interesting because I have a famous mother."

"You must've made quite an impression." Jing grinned. "I think you need to tell me more. What's his name?"

"Corban Abrams. He's from West Fort."

Jing shifted her bag to her other hand. "Abrams? Any relation to Leighton Abrams?"

"Who's he?"

"West Fort's mayor. He showed up at the last council meeting, demanding to speak with our mayor. *Baba* told me about it." Kun Kaczenski was on the Lakeside community council.

"Why did he interrupt? Couldn't he wait to speak to Mayor Brooks in private?"

"Abrams said he wanted all the mayors to meet to discuss the situation with the Strays. He said it was urgent."

"What situation? He sounds like trouble. I hope he's not related to Corban."

"Mayor Brooks told him to shut his mouth and leave, but *Baba*'s interested in what Abrams has to say."

"I don't understand. What do people have against Strays? We're harmless."

"Hate to break it to you, if you haven't noticed, but most Survivors don't think Strays are harmless. I'm not a Stray, but I don't have a problem living in close proximity." Jing flashed a grin. "Why do you think that is?"

"It must be a generational thing. Strays get along fine with other Strays. And Normals like you don't mind us. It's the Survivors who look at me like I'm going to burn their crops and kidnap their children. I'm surprised they haven't made us paint *S*'s on our foreheads so they know who to avoid."

"Your mother's a Survivor, but she likes Strays," Jing said.

"Mom's the reason Vesta has any Survivors." Nikki shook her head. "I think it's natural for parents to love their children, even if they're strange."

Jing frowned. "Not all of them. *Baba*'s happy Zhao is old enough to move out and live with the Mechanics Guild. He's been telling Zhao to leave since he turned eighteen."

"But Zhao's one of the nicest people I know. What does your father have against him?"

"Just his Talent."

"I don't even know what it is," Nikki said. "I thought he was Normal, like you."

Jing hesitated a moment before explaining. "Zhao can touch anything and tell you who touched it last. If it's a chair, he can tell you which carpenter made it. He can tell you every person who *sat* in the chair since its creation."

Nikki wasn't concerned by her revelation. "Sounds like he'd make a good detective."

"It makes *Baba* so uncomfortable, he doesn't want to be seen with Zhao in public. His own son!" Jing bounced her bag against her thigh. "They've been arguing about it for months. I'm sure the neighbors know about Zhao's Talent by now."

"Get out the torches and pitchforks?" Nikki said.

"What are you talking about?"

"It's from an old Earth book about monsters."

"Strays aren't monsters." They reached the bridge and headed across the Cold River. "Zhao's my brother, you're my best friend, half our classmates are Strays. It's wrong for people like *Baba* and Mayor Abrams to treat Strays different."

Nikki shrugged. "It's the way it's always been. I'm used to it."

"You shouldn't have to be used to it," Jing said. "Everyone has something to contribute, and we need each other. There's no room for discrimination in a small colony."

"Tell that to Mayor Abrams."

They reached the foot of the gangway and climbed up to the library ship's airlock.

Nikki tapped the public entry code into the keypad and the round door rotated open, admitting them into the bare antechamber. Like all the other ships

66

except the hospital, the library had been stripped to the girders, leaving bulkhead walls, bare steel floors, and a central ladder to the upper decks. She slung her bag over her shoulder and ascended after Jing to the fourth level, which was the only deck left intact for colonists' use.

The library level offered three round study tables, six datafile stations, and a few threadbare couches. It was neither comfortable nor inviting, so it was usually unoccupied whenever Jing and Nikki arrived, except for today.

"Hello, Nikki." Corban rose to his feet to greet them, but she discerned from his sour expression he wasn't pleased she brought someone with her.

"Corban, this is my best friend, Jing Kaczenski. She's Normal."

"You say that like I have slime worms," Jing hissed at Nikki's back.

Nikki shot Jing a warning frown over her shoulder before settling into a chair at Corban's table with a flirtatious smile. "How did you do on your biology paper?"

Jing eyed the open seats at the table, but made a detour to one of the datafile stations and sat with her back to them. It was less awkward, but Nikki knew she would be able to hear every word of her conversation with Corban.

"I don't know my grade yet." He leaned back in his chair, looking more at ease.

"Any new dreams?" Nikki asked.

Corban's relaxed grin vanished. "I can't tell you, not yet."

"Why not?" Nikki didn't want to sound defensive, but her curiosity was piqued.

"It's personal and I don't know you well. Yet."

Nikki noted the pause in his reply, but she was already tired of the evasive answers. "If it's because you want to know about my Talent—"

"No, I wasn't trying to pry."

She didn't know whether to believe him or not but opted to change the subject. "Jing said the mayor of West Fort's named Abrams. Is he any relation?"

The edges of Corban's mouth turned down. "He's my uncle."

"The one who's raising you? You mentioned he was ashamed of your Talent."

"That's the one." His frown became a scowl. "Although he didn't really raise me and Thane. Uncle hired a nanny to take care of us when we were little. Her name's Aliza. Aliza Yarborough. When Thane turned twelve, he dismissed Aliza and expected us to look after ourselves. We live with him because there's nowhere else we can go right now."

"That's so sad." She traced the wood grain of the tabletop with her fingertips, hesitant to continue this line of query. "Do you still see Aliza?"

Corban shifted his gaze from her face to the tattered biology textbook open in front of him on the table. "No, she's married and lives in Greenfield now."

Time to change the subject again. "Tell me about your brother."

"Thane is twenty." Corban raised his eyes to meet hers again. "Don't tell him I said this, but I don't know what I'd do without him. He's looked after me my whole life, and he has the scars to prove it."

"What do you mean? What scars?"

"A night terror took a bite out of his leg when he went outside the gates one night to find me."

"What were you doing outside the gates?"

Corban's brow furrowed. "I don't know. My memory of that night's a blur, to tell the truth."

Nikki almost wished she could see that memory. Almost. "I guess you both made it back inside safe?"

"Safe? No, but lucky to be alive. Thane couldn't hunt anymore, so he switched to the Smiths Guild after his leg healed enough that he could walk again." A flash of guilt crossed Corban's features, but he was quick to change the subject. "His Talent is hearing."

Nikki was intrigued. "How far away can he hear things?"

"He estimates two kilometers." Corban grinned. "It's been useful at times."

"My brother-in-law Derek can send mental messages, but he doesn't have a limit on how far away the recipient has to be."

"Thane's friend, Rupert, can do that too. I wonder how many Strays can send thoughts. It could be useful for communicating between the forts."

"The Stray directory in the datafiles doesn't say who can do what, but I agree it'd be good to have a way to communicate long-distance. I miss being able to pick up a com and call someone."

"Does your sister have a Talent?"

"Yes, math."

Corban nodded. "I need that one."

"Eliana's a human calculator. She should be in the Teachers Guild, but they don't want any Strays corrupting their children in the classroom."

Corban made a sympathetic noise. "Which guild is she in?"

"The same as Derek—merchants. He mentally sends orders to the craft guilds in the other forts—

the few willing to work with Strays. She takes care of the accounts. It's beneath her skills, but their business in Lakeside is doing well. And they had a baby last week, so Travis is keeping her busy."

"You have a nephew?" He raised an eyebrow at her. "It must be nice to have a supportive family."

"You have Thane."

"He's in a different guild. We won't be able to stay together once I turn eighteen."

"You could join his guild, unless you like being a hunter."

"Hate it, actually." Corban shifted in his chair. "But I'm not interested in being a metal-smith, either. I'd like to join the medics, but I heard it's difficult to get an apprenticeship if your family's not in it. I don't have the grades to apply."

She felt a pang of sympathy. "Where will you go?"

"Do you think the herbalists would accept me?" He managed a half-grin, his tone hopeful. "I learned to identify native plants because I spend so much time in the woods, hunting bluedeer. I know the medics depend on the herbalists for medicines, so it'd be a good way to learn about both guilds."

Nikki nodded. "My mother's a guild partner, so she'd be the one to ask. Do you want to discuss it with her?"

"That would be—"

"Don't forget my father's guild master." Jing turned around in her chair to face them. "You know how Kun feels about Strays. He forced out Zhao, his own son."

Corban and Nikki exchanged a startled glance. She forgot Jing was in the room.

"You'd have an easier time if you stayed with the hunters," Jing said.

"I don't want to be a hunter, and I didn't ask for your opinion." Corban's tone turned frosty. He got to his feet and shoved his books into his backpack. "I need to go. It was nice to see you, Nikki." He reached for her hand.

Without thinking, Nikki moved her hand from the table to her lap before he made contact.

"I see how it is." He shot Jing a scowl. "That's why you brought a friend?"

"No, that's not how it is!" Nikki was on her feet, sending a *help me* expression Jing's way. "Please don't leave!"

He shouldered his backpack and headed for the ladder.

"Corban!" Nikki called after him.

"You can't touch her!" Jing bellowed. "No one can touch her! It's not you—it's her stupid Talent!"

Corban froze in his tracks, Nikki's cheeks turned red, and both turned to face Jing.

"Not now, Jing—" Nikki hissed.

"What did you say?" Corban asked.

"She pulled away because she can't touch anyone. It has nothing to do with you, so don't take it personally," Jing explained in a rush. "Tell him about your Talent, Nik."

Nikki shook her head, trying to ignore the block of ice taking up residence in her stomach.

"Tell him!" Jing's tone turned bossy. "He needs to know."

Corban shifted his backpack to the floor and turned his expectant gaze on Nikki.

Nikki couldn't make eye contact with either of them. "I'm . . . telepathic."

"What?" Corban asked.

"I can see a person's memories, but only if I touch them. Any contact triggers it." Nikki bit her lip and raised her eyes to meet his. "My Talent gravitates straight to the dark memories, making me relive all the pain in someone's past. Pulling away is a protective reflex."

She hoped to see a flicker of acceptance in his eyes. The scowl was gone, but what remained was an odd mixture of sympathy and fear. She was grateful Jing kept quiet.

After a lengthy pause, Corban broke the silence. "Could I meet with your mother about joining the guild?"

Nikki nodded, casting Jing a defiant frown. "Our address is 26S, in the south wall. She's always there after midday."

"Thank you. Maybe I'll see you again in a few days." Corban looked over at Jing, his mouth twisted to one side as if he wanted to say more but thought better of it. He turned back to the ladder without another word and descended out of sight.

Nikki waited until they couldn't hear his footsteps on the rungs before rounding on her friend. "Jing!"

"What? I did you a favor!"

EIGHT
GUILD ADVICE

Corban was lost in darkness. He bumped into something tall and solid, which triggered a memory. *Shelves built into the wall.* His fingers encountered stacks of bowls and plates on the shelves, but he was careful not to disturb anything until he got his bearings. It was crucial he made his way through the darkness in silence, although he didn't recall the reason why.

From his experience with kitchen duty, Corban knew the shelving unit spanned the entire length of the room. He used the edge of a shelf as a guide to move forward without stumbling on the stone floor.

The shelf ended without warning, and Corban found himself floundering for a new anchor. His toe encountered the leg of a work table, and he bit his lip to stifle a yelp of pain. He hopped up and down on his uninjured foot until his toe stopped throbbing. *Don't get distracted. Keep searching.*

But what am I looking for? He didn't know why he was in the dining hall in the middle of the night. Since he wasn't hungry, he knew food wasn't the reason.

Don't get caught, was the only thought that made any sense.

Corban maneuvered his way around the long worktable and found another wall. A swift examination with his hands brought him in contact with a doorknob. He turned the handle and pulled open the heavy door. The long, grating squeak of hinges broke the silence like a clap of thunder. Corban tensed and listened, his heart pounding.

Everything was quiet. He slowed his breathing as he slipped inside the pitch-dark pantry. He smelled potatoes and onions. As he stepped inside the room, hands out to prevent himself from bumping into anything else, he heard a new sound.

The wooden floor creaked beneath his feet. He couldn't move silently anymore, as he'd managed on the stone floor. He paused, holding his breath as he listened.

The hairs on the back of Corban's neck stood on end as he heard a soft tapping directly below him.

He dropped to his knees and swept his hands back and forth across the rough floorboards, searching. He found a hinge, which helped him locate the outline of a trapdoor running perpendicular to the floorboards. Following the edge of the trapdoor, he discovered the handle. It was an iron ring, level with the floor.

Also level with the floor was a long iron bar, which ran through the ring, securing it to the floorboards on either side of the handle. The trapdoor couldn't be lifted from above or raised from below with the iron bar in place. Corban dug his index fingers into the narrow slot that secured the bar and pushed it to the left. It wouldn't budge. He tried forcing it to the right, and it moved, freeing the ring.

Corban pried up the handle, gripped it in both hands, and lifted the heavy trapdoor.

***

He sat up too fast in his hammock, and it dumped him onto the floor. It took Corban a moment to realize he had been dreaming. He blinked hard, adjusting his vision to the semi-darkness of his bedroom. As he climbed to his feet, rubbing his skinned knees, he looked out the window. The sky was turning pink; it was almost dawn.

"Thane?"

No answer. His brother's hammock was empty. Thane was at the smithy, doing extra work to convince Chaim Rajamani to keep him in the guild. Corban felt guilty since he was the reason Thane missed work the other day. Now the poor guy was up before Ilios.

Corban showered and got ready for school. He stopped by the dining hall for a plum and piece of toast, and was one of the first students to arrive at school.

His biology teacher, Emily Vaughn, stared at him in surprise. "You're early, Mr. Abrams, first time this semester." Dark-skinned, petite, and gray-haired, but with sharp brown eyes that didn't miss a thing behind wire-rimmed glasses, Ms. Vaughn was one of the few teachers who treated Strays and Normals with equal respect. "I could give you partial credit on the Zegarellium paper if you have it today."

Corban avoided her gaze. "Sorry."

"A good grade in my class would help on your apprenticeship application. Which guild were you considering? Staying with the hunters?"

"No, I'm thinking about the herbalists."

"Exactly why you need a good grade in biology." Ms. Vaughn turned to greet the other students as they trickled into the classroom.

Corban thought about Ms. Vaughn's advice. The idea of being in the same guild with Nikki Ramirez motivated him to do something he normally avoided—homework. He found a blank sheet of paper in his backpack and spent the entire class writing down what he remembered about Zegarellium from his first encounter with Nikki in the library. He knew he should have been listening to Ms. Vaughn, but he looked up often to act like he was paying attention.

On the way out of biology, he handed Ms. Vaughn the paper with a sheepish grin.

She narrowed her eyes at him with a suspicious frown. "This gives you a solid D for the course, Mr. Abrams, unless you do well on the final exam."

"Yes, ma'am. I'll try."

He attempted to pay attention in his other three classes, advanced math, Earth history, and Common composition, but it was a relief to be done for the school day. Instead of going back to the apartment or stopping by the smithy to see if Thane wanted to break for lunch, he headed to the fortress gates.

It was six kilometers to Lakeside. He encountered more vehicle than foot traffic on the road. A few trucks passed him, heading toward West Fort with the usual shipments of produce for the dining hall. Corban stepped onto the shoulder to allow a flatbed truck loaded with stones to pass him. It wasn't unusual to see lumber trucks coming from the sawmill after a storm, due to needed repairs, but it was odd to see trucks carrying large stones from the quarry unless something new was being constructed. Corban watched the flatbed take the right fork ahead of him and head toward Waterfall. *More stones for the new fort?* He put the thought out of his mind as he hurried past the three-trunked tree, avoiding the cache as Thane advised.

Half an hour later, he walked beneath the archway gate to Lakeside and found his way to Nikki's apartment. He was perspiring from the long hike, but forgot to bring a clean shirt to change into. *Let's hope I don't smell like a night terror.* He knocked on the whitewashed door with *26S* carved into the upper panel.

"You must be Corban. Nikki told me to expect you." The woman who opened the door was a head shorter than Nikki. Her reddish hair was streaked with gray but she had a youthful face, except for her large brown eyes which appeared to belong on a much older woman.

Corban was awestruck by Solona Zegarelli, the wo-man who became Vesta-Lambda colony's accidental savior. Unable to get his mouth to cooperate, he stuck out his hand to shake hers, realized his palm was sweaty, snatched it back, wiped it dry on the leg of his jeans, and offered it again, to her amusement.

She gripped his hand and used it to draw him inside the apartment. "Come in, sit down. You look hot. Let me get you some water."

"Thank you," he managed to squeak. Corban's eyes swept the sitting room, hoping to see Nikki, but she wasn't home. The room was filled with leafy plants growing in clay pots near the windows and tied in bundles left to dry on the exposed beam across the ceiling. He recognized the scent of lavender, but most of the other plant smells were too subtle to identify.

Ms. Zegarelli handed Corban a ceramic cup of cold water. "I'm surprised to see you here. Nikki said she was going over to West Fort to see you today."

Corban sank into a chair and drained the cup. "I didn't see her on the way."

"She must've gone to the library with Jing. Maybe you'll see her when you go back." She settled into a tattered loveseat across from him. "Now, what can I do for you?"

"I want to apply to your guild as an apprentice."

Ms. Zegarelli offered him a cautious smile. "Nikki told you your application would have to go through Kun Kaczenski, Jing's father?"

Corban nodded. "Does he need to know I'm a Stray?"

"I think he'd find out if you try to deceive him. It might ruin your chances of being accepted into the guild."

Corban frowned. "Whether I admit I'm a Stray or not, it sounds like my chances of getting in aren't good."

"Why the sudden interest in the herbalists? Don't you have friends in other guilds?"

He thought a moment. "There's Malachi al-Abdullah. He goes hunting with me sometimes even though he's in the Textiles Guild. And Rupert Conquist . . . he's in the smiths." Corban shook his head. "Actually, he's my brother's friend." He sighed and admitted, "I don't have many friends."

"I want to be sure your newfound interest in the herbalists isn't an attempt to impress my daughter."

Corban appreciated her direct manner, even if it made him squirm. "No, ma'am. I've always been

78

interested in plants." *Although you wouldn't know it by looking at my science grades.* "I'd like to be in the medics, but I know it's hard to get in. I thought I'd be able to learn about medicine through the Herbalists Guild. Isn't that the route your career took, ma'am?"

She grimaced. "You can dispense with the 'ma'am' nonsense. It's just Solona, please."

He nodded. "But since you mentioned Nikki—"

She narrowed her eyes at him. "What about her?"

"Do you mind if I ask her out?" Corban asked.

Solona leaned back in her chair. He sensed apprehension behind her smile. "I think you'd find an untouchable relationship disappointing, but you're welcome to see her as often as you like." She tilted her head, as if to study him from a different angle. "Just try not to break her heart."

Corban didn't know what to say, and his face must have shown it.

"I guess you don't know about her Talent."

"No, ma'—Solona. Nikki told me about it." *Under pressure from Jing, but she did tell me.* "I don't understand how it works, but I do know how tough it is to have a Talent that makes life difficult."

Solona nodded but didn't press him for an explanation. He sensed approval, but the fear remained. It took him a moment to discern that she wasn't nervous about Nikki. She was concerned about something else, something big.

"I hope you see Nikki at West Fort. It'd be a shame if she walked all the way over there and you missed each other."

Corban took that as an invitation to leave and got to his feet, handing her the empty cup. "If I apply to the guild, would you put in a good word for me with Mr. Kaczenski?"

"Of course." Solona ushered him to the door. "Thanks for coming by, Corban. It was nice to meet you."

***

Corban stopped by the library ship before heading back to West Fort. The fourth floor was empty. He didn't see Nikki on the walk back, and there was no note to indicate she stopped by the Abrams's apartment.

As he and Thane sat down to dinner, Corban voiced his concern. "How is it I walked to Lakeside and she walked to West Fort, but we missed each other?"

"She probably changed her mind and went somewhere else after the library."

Corban tapped a roll against the edge of his plate. He needed to tell Thane Nikki was the girl from his dream, but there was no easy way to do it. "So remember my premonition about the girl with the sword?"

Thane looked askance at him. "Darkness. You're joking—Nikki's the girl who's going to kill you?"

Corban nodded.

"Are you out of your mind?"

"Shhh, keep it down. Yes, I'm insane. I thought you knew."

"Have you told her about the premonition?"

"I should probably save it for the second date. 'I dreamt you cut off my head with my uncle's sword' doesn't sound too romantic."

Thane's laugh was humorless. "You're seriously attracted to her? Do you have a death wish?"

"Wait until you hear about her Talent."

"Does it have something to do with decapitating people?"

Corban ignored the sarcasm. "No, she's telepathic."

Thane blew out a long breath. "Poor girl."

"There's more," Corban said. "She can't touch anyone because physical contact triggers her Talent. She said it's like reliving all their darkest memories."

"You're seriously attracted to her?" Thane shook his head. "You can't touch her and she's going to kill you? Everything you'd want in a girlfriend."

"We don't know she's going to kill me." Corban ignored the girlfriend remark.

"You saw it in your premonition. I don't know too many people who've had their heads cut off and lived to tell about it." Thane covered his eyes with one hand. "I can't believe we're having this conversation. I don't understand any of this."

Corban didn't understand it either, but he felt better for having shared it with Thane. "Did you overhear any interesting conversations today?"

"Don't change the subject." Thane glared at him for a full minute before throwing up his hands in defeat. "This is crazy. We'll discuss it later, after I've had time to think. As for listening today, I didn't. I focused on my work. It takes concentration to eavesdrop, and I wanted to make Chaim's quota."

"Is he treating you any better?"

Thane rolled his eyes in response. "He hasn't criticized me as much as he normally does, so I think it's the best I can do for now. How about you? Any new premonitions?"

Corban hesitated, glancing over at the swinging door to the kitchen. "I'm not sure."

Thane followed his gaze. "Reminiscing about kitchen duty? You're welcome to take my next shift."

"No, I don't know why I'd be sneaking around here in the middle of the night."

"Here? In the dining hall?" Thane arched an eyebrow at him. "You had a premonition about coming here in the middle of the night?"

Corban nodded.

Thane snorted. "Your dreams are getting weirder. Maybe Nikki will show up and try to drown you in the vinegar barrel."

"She wasn't in my dream. I heard tapping under the floor of the pantry. Someone was down there, I think. I pulled up the trapdoor, but then I woke up."

"What night were you planning to investigate the pantry?"

"I have no idea! It could be months from now. I have the most useless Talent in the colony."

"No, I think Nikki holds that title."

Corban lapsed into silence, thinking of his recent premonition. "Too bad she can't read Uncle's mind and tell us what he's up to. It'd save you lots of eavesdropping."

Thane's expression darkened. "I hope she never gets within two kilometers of him."

NINE
BLUEPRINTS

"You're not going to West Fort alone." It wasn't a question.

"I'll be fine, Jing. I'm just stopping by Corban's apartment."

"Stopping by to do what?" Nikki knew Jing was angry by the way she was banging her school bag against her thigh. "You might run into the mayor."

"I want to talk to Corban. It's the middle of the day, I'm sure his Uncle won't be home." Nikki stopped on the bridge and moved over to rest her elbows on the railing. She stared down at the river, her mind churning like the choppy gray water.

"Leighton Abrams is dangerous. No Stray should go near that man." Jing joined her at the railing.

"So I won't go near him."

"Corban said he'd stop by to talk to your mom. Be patient. You'll see him soon enough."

"Do you think I have a chance, now that he knows?"

"You're not still mad at me?" Jing turned to give Nikki a pitiful pout.

"Of course, I'm still mad. It was too much information, too soon."

"You were talking about Talents," Jing said. "It was going to come up sooner or later."

"You didn't have to be rude."

"Were you going to explain to him why you snatched your hand away?" Jing scrutinized Nikki's face. "No? I didn't think so."

Too frustrated to reply, Nikki shouldered her school bag, and they resumed their walk toward the library ship. "Do you think he'll want to see me again, now that he knows we can never even hold hands?"

"Friendship first," Jing said. "Don't rush the romantic stuff. It never turns out well."

"Just because Isaac Nomura stood you up for the guild formal last storm doesn't mean every romance is doomed."

"Isaac didn't stand me up. *Baba* found out he was a Stray and threatened to cut off his ears with the hedge clippers if he came near me. He was too scared to take me to the dance."

Nikki grinned. "Was it his ears? I thought it was something lower."

"Darkness! I can't believe you said that!"

Stopping at the foot of the gangway to the ship, Nikki turned to Jing with a serious expression. "I think I should go now so I can get home before dark. Would you take my bag?"

Jing accepted Nikki's backpack with a disapproving scowl. "Are you sure I can't go with you?"

"Positive. I don't need a chaperone this time."

"I think he'd prefer not to see me again." Jing nodded. "But please be careful."

Nikki turned back toward the bridge. "I will."

***

It was four kilometers to West Fort from the landing strip. Half a dozen delivery vehicles passed her along the way, but no other pedestrians. An elderly fisherwoman on a bike offered to give her a ride, but Nikki eyed the flopping celadon trout in the tow cart and politely declined. She wasn't sure if the woman was strong enough to peddle herself the rest of the way. Plus, Nikki didn't want to share the tiny space with a cartload of smelly fish.

As she approached the fortress gates, Nikki recalled she didn't have Corban's address. Although she hoped to be discreet, she needed to ask someone for directions.

The gate sentry appeared to be a safe bet. She was an older woman who looked bored to the point of falling asleep at her post. The embroidered name badge on her faded navy blue uniform said *L. O'Rourke.*

"Could you tell me where Mayor Abrams lives?" Nikki asked.

"Why?" O'Rourke shifted her staff to her other hand and glared up at Nikki—who was taller than most women—with a suspicious frown.

"I have a message for him," Nikki said.

"From who?"

Nikki thought the sentry was being nosy, but she continued with the ruse. "The mayor of Lakeside. Something about a meeting."

She was surprised O'Rourke accepted her explanation with a nod. "Abrams lives in the third floor northwest corner apartment, 30W."

"Thank you." Nikki turned to head inside the fort.

"He won't be in," O'Rourke said. "He usually visits the construction site every day."

"What construction site?" Nikki looked back at the sentry with a puzzled frown.

"Seventh Fort."

"I thought it was still being planned."

The sentry's grin was smug. "Mayor Abrams has his reasons for not sharing this information yet."

Nikki pasted on a fake smile. "Is it a surprise?"

"Yes, and it will remain a surprise until he's ready to announce it." O'Rourke gave her a stern look.

"Yes, ma'am, you have my word. I'll just slip the message under his door. Thank you." Nikki continued through the archway onto the main street. Despite the warmth of the afternoon, she felt cold. *Why is Abrams keeping the work on Seventh Fort a secret?*

Nikki had been to West Fort once to assist her mother with a home birth, but she couldn't recall specific details of the settlement's layout. She studied a signpost to get her bearings. It was a directional sign, stating *East Wall* and pointing back toward the gate. She turned north and followed the cobblestone street that bordered the fortress wall.

West Fort's layout was similar to Lakeside's. Both were square and organized in grids with cobbled streets. Log- and stone-constructed townhomes filled the courtyard space and three-story stone apartment buildings formed the exterior walls. Two signposts at the first intersection pointed to the left, *Market Square* and *Community Chapel*. A few more intersections brought her to *North Wall* and *West Fort Community School*, which was a large stone building. Since the school appeared deserted, she assumed classes were over at midday like hers.

A dining hall was across the street from the school. The double doors were propped open, and the aroma of fresh baked bread made Nikki's stomach growl.

"You don't work, you don't eat!" A woman's shrill voice carried from inside. "Now get back to work on those fish!" A disgruntled-looking boy in his early teens emerged from the kitchen, carrying a large wooden bucket of wriggling fish which might have come straight from the old fisherwoman's cart. He set his load down in front of the doors, took out a cleaver and cutting board, and hacked the head and tail off the first fish.

Nikki lost her appetite when the bright green fish head bounced across the road and came to rest near her, its glassy eyes staring and vacant. She remembered her kitchen duty afternoon was coming up next week and thought about convincing Jing to take her place.

Not a chance. She hates chopping fish as much as I do.

She continued past the school, following the north wall until she came to the intersection of the west wall. The doors at street level led to numbered apartments, and it took her a moment to find the unmarked door to the upper floors. She opened the door to a stone staircase and climbed to the third floor.

Number 30W was across from the stairs, although another door labeled 30W-B was ten meters down the hall to her right. Corner apartments were normally reserved for large families or guild barracks. It was obvious Mayor Abrams pulled some strings to be assigned such a large space. The more Nikki knew about him, the less she liked him.

Now what? She hadn't considered what to do when she reached Corban's apartment. She debated with herself for a moment before walking down to 30W-B and rapping her knuckles on the unfinished wood.

No answer. She knocked again, waited, but when no one came to the door, she took a chance and tried the doorknob.

It was unlocked.

Nikki stepped inside the room and pulled the door shut, her heart pounding against her ribs. "Hello?"

No answer. She was standing in a boys' bedroom. Two hammocks stretched between opposing walls and assorted dirty clothes were strewn across the hardwood floor. The only illumination came from the window. She tiptoed across the room, glancing around with care. An open door led to a bathroom with more dirty clothes on the floor. She hesitated before approaching the other door in the room, which was closed.

Nikki's knock was soft. She was terrified of running into one of the Abramses. She knew she was breaking several laws and couldn't explain what was motivating her curiosity.

No answer. She stepped inside an immaculate room with a huge bed and ornately carved wardrobe, then peered through a doorway into the most opulent bathroom she had ever seen in the colony. *Definitely the mayor's room.*

One more door was left ajar. Nikki listened before tiptoeing into the spacious sitting room, now converted into a community council meeting room. She rotated slowly, taking in every detail of the large oval table and night terror fur rugs. The curtains were drawn so her worry of being seen from someone outside the fort was lessened, although her T-shirt was damp with perspiration from sneaking around where she shouldn't be. A bookcase with stacks of papers organized on the shelves stood against the wall opposite the kitchenette. Some of the papers were rolled up like scrolls.

Like blueprints. Nikki listened again, straining her ears to hear if anyone was outside in the hallway. Someone in the apartment below her was playing a guitar, but she couldn't detect any voices nearby.

She stepped over to the bookcase, picked up one of the scrolls, and unrolled it on the conference table.

Seventh Fort

The scroll contained architect drawings for a stone fortress one hundred meters square—one quarter the size of Lakeside or West Fort. Additional notes were scribbled in random spots in pencil. Nikki squinted to decipher the loopy handwriting. *Guard station.* This was scrawled next to a doorway that opened to the courtyard instead of at the main gates, which was where guards, or sentries, were normally stationed.

The hairs stood up on the back of her neck. Something was strange about this fort. *And isn't Abrams a hunter? Why would he be involved with constructing the new fort?* Nikki rolled up the blueprints and placed them back where she found them. She lifted a sheet of paper from one of the stacks and saw the same loopy handwriting on it.

It was a work order to the Glaziers Guild for one hundred and twenty windows. Nikki wasn't a genius at math like her sister, but she did some rough estimates in her head. *That's half the number needed for a three-story building, one hundred meters square.*

She returned the paper to its spot and picked up the blueprints again. Her sweaty palms warned her not to linger, but her curiosity refused to be satisfied until she counted the windows on the plans.

On closer inspection of the drawings, she bit her lip. The windows were on the inside of the fort. There were no exterior windows. She pushed her damp hair off her forehead. *What in darkness is going on?*

The rattle of the doorknob came without warning. Nikki didn't have a second to hide.

"What are you doing in here?" She had no doubt the man who stormed into the room was Leighton Abrams.

"I was waiting for Corban," was the first thing to pop into her head. "He told me to wait here." With the blueprints in her hand, she knew nothing she said would convince Abrams she was telling the truth.

"Who are you? How did you get in here?" He took a few menacing steps in her direction. "Those are my papers, you thief!"

Nikki scurried around the opposite side of the table to get away from him. "I'm no one. I didn't mean any harm. I'll just put it back and leave."

"I don't think so." He changed directions and came after her around the other side of the table. "Who are you?"

She retreated again, hoping to get closer to one of the doors, but Abrams seized the edge of the table and overturned it. She scrambled backward to get out of the way, but the heavy table grazed her shins and knocked her down. She fell against the bookcase, spilling papers everywhere.

Abrams climbed over the wreckage, reaching for her.

"No! Don't touch me! Please don't touch me!"

He seized her left arm. The images that invaded Nikki's mind were terrifying, filled with anger, fear, and raw hatred. Memories raced past her vision like a holo-vid set to skip ahead from scene to scene.

A younger Corban cowered on the same floor, defending himself from Abrams's fists. She saw another young man with a brace on his leg, pleading with Abrams to leave Corban alone, only to be shoved aside.

Scene change: A bluedeer collapsed from a rifle shot and Abrams stood over the wounded beast, shooting it again and again at point-blank range.

Scene change: an older memory. A younger version of Abrams shouted at a boy who resembled Corban, although he was half the size of the current Corban.

"You left it outside the fort, you worthless Stray! You go get it, right now!"

The younger Corban looked up at his uncle with wide eyes. "But it's almost dark."

"Then you'd better hurry!" Abrams shoved him toward the door. "Run so you can get back inside the gates before they close!"

The child-Corban stared back at his uncle in terror before stumbling out the door of the apartment.

"Now to make sure your worthless Stray brother goes looking for you," Abrams said to himself with a self-satisfied chuckle.

Scene change: Abrams was looking at some rifle cartridges in his hand. "We'll need to make more—"

The scene vanished when present-day Abrams released Nikki's arm.

"What in darkness is wrong with you, Stray?" He spat the word as if it were the vilest profanity.

It took Nikki a moment to get her bearings. Being left alone with her own thoughts after someone else's memories invaded her mind was always disconcerting. She focused on the angry man standing over her, recalling where she was. "I'm sorry! Please let me leave! I promise you'll never see me again!"

Abrams seized her by the hair, and dragged her to her feet. New images filled her mind but she was unable to block them.

"How do you know that? How could you possibly know?" The Abrams in her mind was screaming at Corban.

"I thought you'd be happy to know you'll win." Corban was holding a hand to a cheek turning crimson.

"It's unnatural! You shouldn't be around Normal people! You disgust me!" Abrams shoved his nephew toward the door. "Get out!"

Nikki heard a ripping sound and was dimly aware of something sticky and tight being slapped over her mouth. *Tape?* Her hands were tied behind her back with something thin and rough. *Rope?*

Abrams shoved her to the floor, giving her a break from the mental torture. "Stay there!"

Why isn't anyone coming to investigate? She heard Abrams leave, slamming the door behind him. She didn't hear the guitar anymore. *The musician must have heard my screams and the table overturn.* But no one came.

Nikki opened her eyes. The night terror rug beneath her was spotted with blood. Her elbow was bleeding from the fall into the bookcase, but she hadn't notice it from the adrenaline coursing through her veins.

She struggled to her feet and climbed around an overturned chair, hoping to reach the door which led back to the bedrooms, but she wasn't fast enough.

The door to the hallway burst open and Abrams returned with the sentry O'Rourke on his heels. The older woman's jaw dropped as she surveyed the wrecked room and Nikki, but she didn't say a word.

"Help me get her in the barrel. I want her kept in the cellar."

Barrel? Nikki felt a flicker of horror. What did this madman intend to do with her?

"Yes, sir." O'Rourke stepped into the hall for a moment and returned, rolling a large wooden wine cask ahead of her through the doorway.

Nikki made another attempt to get to the other door, but Abrams swooped down on her and seized her arm again.

She shut her eyes but couldn't block the invasion of Abrams's terrible memories.

"They won't go willingly." Abrams whispered to another man she didn't recognize.

"We'll persuade them," the bald stranger said. "The hunters are already willing to donate their rifles."

"We won't have enough ammo," Abrams said.

"We'll make more—"

A hand gripped her other arm and the scene changed. She saw O'Rourke sitting on the riverbank beside a young boy with a fishing pole. They were laughing. She saw no animosity, no violence like in Abrams's memories. She realized O'Rourke was just doing her job.

"She asked for your address, said she had a message from Lakeside's mayor." O'Rourke's tone was apologetic.

"She's a liar. Can't you see she broke in and was snooping through my papers?" Abrams's grip on Nikki's arm tightened, but thankfully the scene on the riverbank remained in her mind until both adults released her, shoving her head-first into the upright barrel and bending her legs to force them inside.

Nikki banged her head against the bottom, slumped upside-down in an uncomfortable position. She opened her eyes to darkness as the lid was put into place and screwed shut. *I'm going to suffocate!*

The barrel was turned onto its side, and Nikki was confronted with a more urgent problem than suffocation. *They're going to roll me someplace, and if I get dizzy and vomit, I'll asphyxiate with the tape over my mouth!*

Abrams's and O'Rourke's voices outside the barrel were muted. Nikki willed her stomach to remain calm. *Where are they taking me?* She attempted to brace her elbows and knees against the sides of the barrel to prevent from being banged around with each rotation, but she wasn't successful.

Mercifully, they didn't roll her down two flights of stairs but set the barrel upright and carried it. Once at the bottom, she was flipped onto her side again and rolled a long distance. Her stomach churned, but she kept her eyes on a knothole near the lid where a thumbnail-size ray of light came in. It helped keep the nausea at bay.

More muted voices and the scent of baking bread. *The cellar is in the kitchen?* Nikki knew Lakeside had a holding cell near the sentry station where lawbreakers were held for minor infractions such as drunkenness and fighting. Why didn't Abrams put her in a cell?

Unless he doesn't want anyone to know I'm being held prisoner?

Nikki also knew more serious law-breaking resulted in expulsion from the fort at night. Was Abrams planning to wait until nightfall to get rid of her? The thought made her think suffocation wouldn't be so bad.

Suffocation wasn't Abrams's plan, however. The barrel was set upright again, lowered a short distance, and the lid was removed.

O'Rourke was alone as she seized Nikki under the arms, hoisted her out of the barrel, and sat her on a dirt floor. "You'll be fine here, for now, until the mayor decides what to do with you." She didn't make eye contact with Nikki as she stooped beneath the low ceiling to light a small oil lamp and set it on the floor in one corner. "There's a chamber pot." She pointed it out in another corner. "And someone will bring you food and water at dinnertime."

Nikki watched O'Rourke lift the barrel through the trapdoor above their heads, climb up herself, and lower the door, cutting off the light and kitchen noises from above.

She heard a metallic sound of something sliding along the trapdoor, footsteps on the wooden floor a few decimeters above her head, another door closing, and silence.

***

The rope bit into Nikki's wrists as she tried again to loosen her bonds. It was no use. Her skin was raw, and she was barely getting enough blood to her fingertips to keep them from going numb.

95

Her throat was also raw from thirst and from the heavy tape across her mouth. No water remained in the shallow ceramic cup near her left knee, and the matching plate held nothing but crumbs. She stared at the wooden tray, which held the empty dishes. The meager meal had been brought to her hours ago. Her silent guard O'Rourke ripped off the tape and allowed her three bites of bread before holding the cup to her lips for a few desperate gulps of water to chase it down. Then she taped Nikki's mouth again and left her alone.

The weak flame from the oil lamp was shrinking. Soon she would be in total darkness. Nikki's eyelids were heavy, but she didn't relish the thought of lying on the hard-packed floor with nothing but dirt for a pillow. She sat cross-legged in the middle of her prison and wondered how she was going to get out. She looked up at the floorboards, which formed the low ceiling of the cellar, and strained her ears to hear anything. Several times during the day she heard footsteps overhead, but many hours passed since the last floorboard creaked. She knew it must be late. The kitchen staff was gone and she was alone.

Even when you're around people, you're still alone because you're untouchable. She watched the lamp's flame grow smaller until it went out.

The darkness pressed in on her like a thick blanket. She forced herself to breathe through her nose, in and out, one breath at a time, and prayed morning would come soon.

A floorboard overhead creaked.

Nikki made an impulsive decision. *I'm not waiting until morning! I'm getting out of here!*

She shifted until her back was to the dinner tray and scooted backward until she was able to reach it.

Groping with numb fingers, she located the ceramic cup. Nikki gripped the handle and banged the cup against the wooden tray. It wasn't loud, but at least it was noise.

It might be the sentry again, and she's not going to help you. But she hoped it was someone else, someone who didn't know she was being held prisoner in the cellar.

The creaking above her stopped. *Please don't leave me here! Don't leave!*

The trapdoor was raised. She looked up, straining her eyes to see, but it was too dark. She didn't know if the person standing above her thought someone was in the cellar or they were just hearing a noisy rodent. She continued to bang the cup against the tray, breathless with hope.

"Nikki?"

Corban! She dropped the cup. Warm tears stung the corners of her eyes.

"Nikki, I know you're down here. I can sense your presence. Wait a minute, and I'll get a light."

Shaking from a combination of terror and relief, she brought her knees up to her chest, forcing herself to calm down and wait for Corban to return with a lamp.

"Nikki?" Corban lowered himself through the trapdoor. He was barefoot and wearing a stretched-out T-shirt and pajama bottoms. The light from the oil lamp made them both squint. He didn't say anything when he saw her, but his furrowed brow spoke volumes. He crawled on hands and knees to reach her because of the low ceiling. Kneeling on the dirt floor next to her, he murmured, "Sorry," before peeling the tape away from her mouth.

Nikki gasped as the skin around her lips seemed to come away with the tape. She whimpered as Corban moved behind her and sawed through the rope with a kitchen knife he must have picked up when he went to get the lamp. She brought her aching arms in front of her and examined the welts on her wrists, the oozing gash on her elbow.

"Darkness." Corban appeared to be struggling with his own emotions, but he showed real restraint by not touching her.

Nikki turned around to face him, tamping down a desperate need to throw her arms around him and bawl like a baby. "Thank you," was all she managed to whisper.

"Let's get you out of here." He led the way over to the trapdoor.

Nikki crawled after him on shaking hands and knees.

Corban offered a hand but stopped himself before he touched her arm. "Let me help you."

Nikki shook her head. "Don't touch me, please. I can manage." The trapdoor was a meter above the floor so she was able to hoist herself through the opening. On her belly on the pantry floor, she reached down to take the lamp from Corban and moved aside as he climbed up to join her.

"Come on." Corban's frown deepened as he watched her climb unsteadily to her feet.

Nikki understood his frustration. She had spent her entire life unable to touch the people she loved, not even a kiss on the cheek or a handshake. She forced herself not to think about it as she stretched her aching limbs and followed him out of the pantry.

They exited the kitchen and were halfway across the dining room when Nikki spotted a pitcher of water on the buffet table. She made a detour toward it, set the lamp down, raised the pitcher to her mouth, and chugged half the contents before coming up for air.

Corban was at her side. "Darkness. I should've realized you were down there for hours. Let me get you something to eat."

"I'm not hungry,"—which was true, since her stomach was full of water—"just exhausted."

"You mother's worried. She sent me a message. A thought came to my mind a few minutes ago. 'Nikki's missing. She didn't come back from West Fort. Solona needs you to find her.' It was a man's voice."

Nikki nodded. "That was my brother-in-law, Derek."

Corban turned to her with a haunted expression. "I'm so sorry. This is my fault."

"No, I got myself into this mess—" she had been expecting an argument, but didn't get a chance to finish her sentence.

Two people burst into the dining room through the main doors, blocking their exit.

"Uncle!" Corban shouted.

Mayor Abrams was wielding a long sword, but the sentry O'Rourke was unarmed.

Corban motioned for Nikki to get behind him. "What are you doing here?" She thought he was making an effort to sound brave, but his voice went up an octave.

"What are you doing here, Corban, with this criminal?"

"Nikki's not a criminal!"

"You're helping her escape!" Abrams moved toward them with the sword held out in front of him.

"Strays! Sticking your noses where they don't belong." He stopped an arm's length from Corban. "Stand aside. I should have put the thief outside the fort at dusk instead of waiting until now."

Darkness! Nikki was chilled to realize how close she came to being sent to her death.

Corban shouted, "You stay away from her!"

Nikki glanced at Corban's waist, but he didn't have his machete. *We need a weapon!* She shrank back against the buffet table, searching for a knife, preferably a long, sharp one.

The point of Abrams's sword came to rest on the cleft of Corban's chin. "Stand aside, you worthless Stray."

Nikki's fear was replaced with white-hot fury. She grabbed the pitcher and flung the remaining contents over Corban's shoulder, right in the mayor's face.

Corban shoved the sword away from his chin and threw himself at his uncle, who was momentarily blinded by the water. He seized the hilt of the sword, and the two men struggled for possession of it. O'Rourke made no move to intervene, watching the fight with wide-eyed interest.

Abrams punched Corban in the stomach and laughed as his nephew doubled over.

With a cry of rage, Corban sank his teeth into his uncle's right hand. The mayor screamed in pain, dropped the sword, and seized his nephew by the throat with both hands.

"No!" Nikki watched in horror as Corban clawed at Abrams's hands, desperate to break his grip.

TEN
FIGHT AND FLIGHT

Thane didn't hear anything when he was asleep. His subconscious, however, interrupted his slumber whenever Corban spoke. It was an ingrained response, honed by a lifetime of big brother duty.

"Uncle!"

Thane heard the shout as if it was right next to his ear. He sat upright in the hammock and it turned over, dumping him onto the floor. Struggling to his feet, Thane cursed his bad leg and the precious time it would take him to strap on his brace.

Where is he? He kept his ears tuned as he switched on the overhead light and fumbled with the straps of the brace.

Corban's boots and belt with his machete were on the floor near his hammock, so he must have left in a hurry. Thane didn't hear him in the apartment. *Where would he go in the middle of the night?*

The answer came like a bolt of lightning. *The premonition he told me about at dinner!*

"Nikki's not a criminal!"

The shout confirmed the location. Corban was in the dining hall with Nikki and Uncle.

Thane moved as fast as his left leg allowed, hopping down the stairs on his right to save time.

"You stay away from her!"

Using a long skipping stride that put less weight on his bad leg and propelled him down the street faster than normal, Thane headed toward the dining hall, ready to do battle. Many things were becoming clearer in his mind, but he didn't have time to analyze them. He knew Corban heard Nikki in the cellar in his dream, and Uncle put her there. *But how did Corban know she was there tonight? Another premonition?*

He pushed through the double doors into the dining hall, surprising an older female sentry standing inside the doorway. She made a move to block Thane, but he took one look at the scene by the buffet table and shoved her aside.

Leighton was strangling Corban. A young woman clung to Uncle's back, struggling to pull him off Corban, but she appeared to be in a trance, her face frozen in an expression of horror. Uncle let go of Corban long enough to pry her off and shove her to the floor.

Corban emitted a cry of rage and flew at Leighton, managing to land one punch to his jaw before Uncle got both hands around his neck again.

"Stop!" Thane rushed forward and seized Leighton from behind, pulling him off Corban.

"Thane!" Corban sank to the floor, gasping for breath and rubbing his throat.

Leighton broke free of Thane and brought the fight to him. Thane had more upper body strength, but his effectiveness as a fighter was hampered by his bad leg. He managed to get in a few solid punches to

Leighton's face before his uncle head-butted his left shoulder, throwing him off balance. Uncle shoved him to the floor, pinned him on his back, and pounded on him with both fists.

Pain exploded in the center of Thane's face, and he knew his nose had broken. He struggled to block Leighton's blows.

Corban stood over Uncle with something in his hands. There was a *crack* of shattering pottery, and the fight was over. Leighton's eyes rolled up in his head and he slumped, unconscious, next to Thane.

"Mayor Abrams!" The sentry finally showed some interest in the brawl, but Thane ignored her.

Corban was wide-eyed and struggling to breathe as he offered Thane a hand up from the floor, which he accepted. Warm blood poured down Thane's chin but he managed a triumphant grin. It was the first time the brothers fought back, and it felt good.

"Stay where you are. All three of you are under arrest." The sentry came toward them, but Thane noticed she was unarmed.

Nikki moved to block them from the sentry. Thane was shocked to see a sword in her hand. *Leighton's sword!* "Get out of the way, O'Rourke, we're leaving."

The sentry stopped short, her face filled with apprehension as she gave the sword a wide berth. "At least let me check the mayor. Is he dead?"

"We could only be so lucky." Corban offered Thane a napkin for his streaming nose and an arm to lean on for support. "Take care of him and don't follow us."

The sentry nodded, eyes on the sword, and waited until they passed her before bending over Abrams.

Nikki led the way out of the dining room. The street was deserted, although Thane thought the fight was loud enough to wake someone.

"We need to get out of West Fort," she said. "When your uncle recovers, he'll come after all of us."

"Let's grab some things from our room first," Corban said.

Thane blotted his streaming nose, which turned his beard and the front of his shirt crimson. "We need to hide until dawn. Let's go to Rupert's."

"That's the first place Uncle will look," Corban said.

"You must be Nikki." Thane made a half-hearted attempt to ease the tension. "It's nice to meet you."

Nikki didn't crack a smile. She shot him a worried look and said, "We need to hurry." She followed the brothers back to their apartment and waited for them in the hallway as they dressed and threw a few belongings into their backpacks.

"She's got Uncle's sword." Thane snatched a washcloth next to the sink and held it to his gushing nose.

"I know." Corban reached around Thane to grab his toothbrush. "We'll have to discuss it later."

"How did you know she was in the cellar?"

"I said later." Corban cinched the top of his bag shut. "Hurry."

They emerged from the bedroom to join Nikki, who was tapping her foot with impatience. She had improvised a twist of fabric from the hem of her shirt to secure the sword at her side. Her face, arms, and clothes were smeared with dirt, and she was trembling.

Thane reached out to take her arm, but Corban and Nikki said, "Don't touch her!" and "Don't touch me!" in unison.

"Sorry, I forgot. Her Talent?" Thane looked at Corban for confirmation.

Nikki scowled at both of them. "We can discuss it later. My mother should tend to Thane's nose, and I know she's worried about me. Let's go to Lakeside."

"We'll never make it. The night terrors will rip out our throats as soon as we're past the gates. One sword and a couple machetes won't be enough protection." Thane glanced down at his leg brace. "I was lucky to only lose a kneecap last time I ran into one."

Nikki's bottom lip quivered, but her eyes remained dry. "It's my fault you have to leave. I'm sorry."

"Don't be sorry." Thane said, "Uncle showed us tonight he's capable of murder." He shot a worried frown at his brother. "You've done us a favor, probably saved Corban's life."

Corban was quick to squash the tender moment. "We're taking too long. I'm sure Uncle's awake by now—and I hope he has a raging headache. He'll sound the alarm, and we'll be arrested."

"Not if I can help it." Nikki patted the sword at her waist.

The brothers exchanged a nervous glance.

"Let's go." Nikki led the way down the stairs.

"Where are we going?" Corban said. "It won't be dawn for another hour, at least."

"You must know someone your uncle won't search out." Nikki's tone turned impatient. "Come on, think. You've lived here your whole lives." She stopped at the bottom of the stairs, glancing back at them. "I think we'll get caught if we go outside."

"Ms. Vaughn, my biology teacher." Corban's face lit up. "She lives right here, in the west wall."

"Can you trust her?" Nikki turned to Thane.

Thane nodded. "She'll help us."

"Lead the way."

Corban led them back up to the second floor and down the hall to apartment 21W. His knock on the door echoed like a gong in the empty hallway.

It took Ms. Vaughn a few minutes to answer the door. Wrapped in a bathrobe, she greeted them with a cold scowl until she recognized who was standing on her doorstep.

"Mr. Abrams and Mr. Abrams? It's a bit early for a visit. And who is this?" She appraised Nikki with a concerned frown.

"This is Nikki Ramirez," Corban said. "Please, may we come in? We need your help."

"You certainly do." Ms. Vaughn ushered them into her sitting room and shut the door.

Thane opened his mouth to explain, but she took charge of the group. "Mr. Abrams, go to the kitchen and get that bleeding under control. There's ice in the freezer—you'll need it. I don't care how many dish towels you use up. Mr. Abrams," she faced Corban, "you sit here and I'll bring you some ice too. It looks like you have some bruising around your neck. Ms. Ramirez, the bathroom is first door on the left. Take a shower. I'll bring you a bathrobe. Try not to track dirt on my floor."

"Yes, ma'am." Thane almost grinned at Nikki's meek tone.

ELEVEN
FUGITIVES

Corban's neck was cold from the ice packs, but he tolerated the discomfort, grateful to be alive. Ms. Vaughn's couch was comfortable, despite the worn-out springs and threadbare fabric. He wanted to stretch out and close his eyes, but too many questions demanded answers. The most pressing problem was how to get out of West Fort without being seen.

By dawn, all the sentries will be looking for us.

Nikki emerged from the bathroom in a green robe which must have belonged to tiny Ms. Vaughn because it fell to mid-thigh. He repressed the urge to whistle. She sat beside him on the couch, careful to leave a few centimeters of space between them. With her wet hair combed back off her clean face, he saw the bruises for the first time. He glanced at her exposed arms and legs with a fresh surge of anger. Nikki was covered in bruises.

"Darkness. What did he do to you?"

"He caught me looking at the Seventh Fort blueprints in the council room and put me in the cellar without anyone seeing." She rubbed her chafed wrists. "The barrel ride is the reason for the bruises."

Corban's jaw dropped. He needed to ask a dozen follow-up questions, but wasn't sure where to begin. Thane walked out of the kitchen before he opened his mouth.

"It finally stopped bleeding!" His brother joined them on the couch, holding ice packs to his nose and chin. "Where did Ms. Vaughn go?"

"Back to bed?" Corban said. "She didn't leave the apartment."

Ms. Vaughn answered the question by emerging from a door next to the bathroom. "Good, you all look better. I'm sorry I don't have anything to fit you, Ms. Ramirez."

"Please call me Nikki. I can wear this, if you don't mind me borrowing it."

Corban's jaw dropped but he was quick to shut it.

Ms. Vaughn shot him a warning frown. "I was about to say my daughter's clothes might fit you. Let's step into the bedroom and find something."

"You have a daughter?" Corban knew nothing about Emily Vaughn's personal life.

Ms. Vaughn smiled. "Brida is my adopted daughter. None of her family survived the Plague, so I took her in."

"I've never seen her at school," Corban said. "Is she our age?"

"She's twenty-five. You've never seen her because she can't leave the apartment. Her Talent makes it impossible for her to go outside."

"I don't understand." Corban didn't mean to pry, but his curiosity got the better of him. "What kind of Talent is so isolating?"

"I'll let her tell you herself." Ms. Vaughn gestured for them to join her.

Corban, Thane, and Nikki followed Ms. Vaughn into a neat bedroom with twin beds and drawn curtains. A small lamp on a nightstand provided the only light. Brida Vaughn—Corban assumed Vaughn was her surname—was sitting up in one of the beds with a dreamy smile. A mop of brown curls framed a pale, round face with heavily lidded eyes and a bow-shaped mouth with the tip of her tongue poking out. She looked much younger than twenty-five.

"Brida, this is Thane, Nikki, and Corban." Ms. Vaughn perched on the bed beside her daughter, who was beaming at them as if she were on a pleasant holiday.

"What's wrong—?" Nikki's voice was soft.

"Brida has Down syndrome," Ms. Vaughn explained. "It's a rare condition."

Corban was confused. "Is that her Talent?" He had never sensed someone so happy. Pure joy radiated from Brida.

"No, she was born with an extra chromosome. It dramatically affected her DNA change when she was exposed to the Plague, giving her an unusual Talent for seeing auras."

"What's an aura?" Thane asked.

Ms. Vaughn turned to Brida. "What do you see?" She gestured to Thane.

"Light," Brida spoke with a lisp in a thick, child-like voice. "I see light around him, but some dark. He has lived with darkness."

Corban exchanged an astonished look with Thane.

"And him?" Ms. Vaughn pointed to Corban.

Brida giggled. "Light from him, too, but he's also lived with darkness. He has darkness he keeps inside. He needs to let it go."

The sharp intake of breath Corban heard was his own.

"And her?" Ms. Vaughn put her arm around Brida's shoulders.

"Light, but she's like me. She can see the darkness and the light."

Nikki's eyes were wide. "No, I can't. I can't detect people's auras or tell what they're thinking by looking at them." She balled her hands into fists. "I only see memories, all of them, good and bad, and I can't control it."

"Sure you can," Brida said. "You just have to choose."

"Choose what?" Nikki sounded rattled, and Corban didn't blame her.

"Choose what you want to see." Brida stared at Nikki before turning her gaze on Corban again. "Your light is the same as hers."

"What does that mean?" Nikki shot Corban a scowl, as if he knew what Brida was talking about.

"It means you share the same light." Brida grinned, as if that explained everything. "Nice to meet you all."

Ms. Vaughn got to her feet. "And that's our cue to leave."

Corban wanted to ask more questions, but he backed out of the room with Thane and Nikki. They avoided eye contact, lost in their own confused thoughts, and returned to the couch. Ms. Vaughn emerged a minute later with some clothes for Nikki.

"I still don't understand," Thane said. "Why can't Brida leave the apartment?"

"Because dark auras upset her."

Corban still didn't grasp what an aura was. "How many people have dark auras?"

"People who don't like Strays."

Nikki pursed her lips. "So lots of people."

Ms. Vaughn nodded. "Here, try these on, Nikki. Then let's figure out how to smuggle you three out of West Fort."

Corban didn't know how she knew what they needed, but he made up his mind to be grateful and keep his mouth shut.

***

"Gina will be in the kitchen by now, starting breakfast preparations. Don't leave." Ms. Vaughn fixed Corban and Thane with a stern gaze. "Don't even look out the window. Brida's asleep, so keep your voices down. I'll be right back." She slipped out of the apartment without waiting for another question from the three fugitives.

"Who would've thought Ms. Vaughn and Ms. Piroux were related?" Thane said. "They're polar opposites in personality. How again are they related?"

"Weren't you listening?" Nikki sounded impatient.

Corban managed to hide a smirk at the irony in her words.

"They're sisters-in-law," Nikki said. "Ms. Piroux was married to Ms. Vaughn's step-brother."

"I hope Piroux isn't still mad at me for making a mess of those trout last month," Corban said.

Thane moved from the couch the floor and stretched out his left leg. "She said the tomato sauce I made tasted like purple crawler droppings."

111

Corban laughed, but Nikki didn't even crack a smile.

"My mom's probably frantic by now," she said.

"Did Derek send you a message?" Thane said.

Nikki covered a yawn. "Early last evening he said, 'Where are you? Your mom's worried' but obviously I didn't have a way to respond." She drew her knees up to her chest and wrapped her arms around them. Brida's long-sleeve black T-shirt was too big for her and her jeans were too short, but they hid most of the bruises.

"Ms. Vaughn's in the kitchen," Thane announced, eyes closed in concentration. "She's talking to Ms. Piroux. Sounds like the word is out we assaulted Uncle last night."

"*We* assaulted *him*?" Nikki growled.

"He's posted a reward for our capture, all three of us."

She muttered an obscenity under her breath and lowered her forehead to her knees. Corban assumed she fell asleep, but she jerked her head up after a moment.

"Derek contacted me. He said Mom's organizing a posse to search for me after dawn."

Corban imagined how Uncle might react to a confrontation with Solona Zegarelli, but Nikki put his thought into words. "She'll add a few more lumps to his skull to match the one you gave him."

She scowled. "You should've seen what she did to my father when he said Eliana and I weren't his daughters because we were Strays. Mom grabbed him by the back of his shirt and shoved him out the door. She told him, 'If I ever see you near *my* daughters, I'll put a load of buckshot in your smug face. I'm sorry my discovery saved your worthless life.'"

112

Corban's jaw sagged. "Your petite little mother did that?"

Nikki managed a tired grin. "You don't mess with Solona."

Thane reported on the meeting in the dining hall. "They're commandeering a delivery truck this morning. They're going to load it with"—he looked confused—"they're going to load it with bags of corn for the gristmill?"

"They're going to hide us inside some bags and smuggle us out in the truck," Nikki guessed with a nod of approval.

"It'll never work," Corban said. "The sentries will search all the vehicles coming and going from the fort."

"They've thought of that possibility too," Thane said. "They're planning a distraction."

Corban groaned. "I don't want to hear anymore."

Nikki appeared energized as she retrieved her shoes. "Let's be ready to go."

"If they're going to put us in bags, how're they going to get the bags in the truck? It'll take three men to lift Thane," Corban said.

Thane opened his eyes long enough to roll them at Corban. "Not three men, just one Stray."

"I thought you said no Stray's able to move anything heavier than a chair."

"You don't need telekinesis if you can project an illusion." Thane grinned. "Ms. Piroux said her daughter can make things invisible to the eye for a few seconds."

"It'll be long enough for us to climb in the truck and get inside the bags." Nikki was bouncing on her heels with impatience. "They can back the truck up to the stairwell of the building."

"Maybe," Corban said, "it might work if we can pull it off before daybreak. Are any trucks not kept at the warehouse overnight?"

Thane frowned. "Uncle's."

Nikki frowned too. "How does he have permission to use a vehicle when there's a shortage?"

"Now you understand the scope of his influence," Thane said.

She snorted. "I understood when I saw the blueprints for Seventh Fort and noticed something odd about it, like no exterior windows."

"I noticed that too. And what's stranger is the fort's almost complete," Thane said.

Nikki looked askance at him. "You knew?"

"Not until I saw it a few days ago," Thane said. "I've eavesdropped on most of the community council meetings but never heard the fort mentioned."

"You were wrong then," Corban told Thane, "Uncle does remember your Talent. He's managed to keep the construction a secret for months."

"But either of you could've seen the blueprints," Nikki said. "Don't you ever go in the conference room, in your own apartment?"

It was Corban's turn to frown. "It's off limits." It was a lame excuse, but it was the truth. "We're not allowed into his section of the apartment, not since he was elected mayor."

Nikki gave him an odd look before speaking. "But I saw you there, in one of his memories. He was . . ." She flushed and turned away.

"He was beating the darkness out of me." Corban was embarrassed, yet he also wanted her to know. *I guess she already knows.* He shifted in his seat at that uncomfortable thought and looked at his feet. "You must think I'm a coward."

"No, you stood up to your uncle to protect me." Nikki's gaze shifted to Thane. "Both of you."

"We should've fought back a long time ago," Thane said. "It's the only way to deal with a bully."

"This was my fault because I shouldn't have been there." Nikki's face was growing pinker. "I'm not sure why I decided to snoop in your apartment. I wasn't planning to, but the door was unlocked—"

Corban sensed her embarrassment. "I would've done the same thing."

"You would've broken in," Thane said.

Nikki giggled. It was the first time Corban heard her laugh, but before he was able to reply, her tone turned somber.

"How did you know I was in the cellar?"

"Premonition," Corban said. "I'm ashamed to admit I had the dream the night before last. You were already in the cellar when I went to bed last night. If Derek didn't wake me with his message, I would've left you there all night."

"But you didn't. You saved my life." She focused on Corban with her mesmerizing brown eyes, her expression undecipherable, but the emotions he sensed were powerful—fear, anger, sympathy. "I can't believe you lived with so much abuse. From what I saw in his memories, I think we're all in danger now that he has some power."

Corban and Thane exchanged an uncomfortable frown. Neither spoke.

"I have an idea what he's planning with Seventh Fort." Nikki rested both hands on the hilt of the sword at her waist. "He has to be stopped."

"Ms. Vaughn's on her way back." Thane struggled to his feet. "And Ms. Piroux's telling her kitchen staff to load the truck with the bags of corn."

***

The sacks were made of burlap, so breathing wasn't an issue, but Corban wrestled with his anxiety of being in an enclosed space. The fabric was scratchy against his arms and face, but it was the dust from the grain that concerned him. He willed himself not to sneeze.

Thane flopped down next to him in the truck bed but Corban didn't know where Nikki was lying in their rush to get inside the sacks. They tucked their knees to their chins to fit in the short bags, which was uncomfortable for Thane. Corban hoped they didn't have to be in the truck for more than a few minutes.

"We're putting some bags on top of you," Ms. Piroux whispered. "They'll hide your shapes better."

"Thank you." Nikki's quiet voice came from somewhere near Corban's feet.

He suppressed a grunt of surprise as a heavy sack of corn landed on his legs. Another one landed on his back. He heard several more thumps and assumed the truck bed was now full.

"Dagmar has your backpacks and sword under the seat. She'll find a deserted spot to let you out of the truck," Ms. Piroux said. "She'll use her Talent again, if necessary. Good luck."

Corban forced himself to slow his breathing to fight off the growing sense of claustrophobia. He heard the truck engine rumble to life and they were moving. A scant minute later, the truck slowed and stopped.

"Destination?" a bored male voice asked.

"Gristmill," a stern, Piroux-like voice answered with confidence.

"Why so much corn?" a different male voice spoke up.

"Ma wants to make cornbread," Dagmar said. "Don't you like cornbread?"

"Abrams wants us to search every vehicle," the first sentry said.

"Hurry up," Dagmar said.

Corban held his breath as he heard footsteps and hands slapping bags. The sentries took a few seconds to check the truck bed.

"It's fine." The second sentry muttered under his breath, "This is a waste of time."

"You're clear," the first sentry said to the driver.

Corban relaxed when the truck began to move again, taking them outside the gates of West Fort. *We can never go back.* A pang of remorse nudged him. *We're banished.*

TWELVE
REUNION

It was an hour after dawn when Nikki opened the door to her mother's apartment and walked in with Corban and Thane on her heels. She knew her family waited up all night for her return, but she wasn't prepared for such an enthusiastic response.

"You're safe!" Jing let out a screech and swooped down on her, enveloping her in a hug.

Nikki went rigid as a flurry of her best friend's memories invaded her mind. She witnessed a shouting match between Jing and her father, but she didn't hear more than a few words before they both disappeared.

Jing released her with a heartfelt, "Sorry!"

Solona catapulted from the bedroom and smothered Nikki in an embrace of her own. Her mother's memories were darker than Jing's and one, in particular, became clear in her mind. Nikki saw a pile of bright purple Zegarellium roots on a table and heard Solona's worried voice whisper, "Long-term side effects," but the memory vanished as abruptly as it began.

"Ouch," Nikki said when her mother released her. "You've never hugged me before."

"You've never gone missing!" Solona turned to Corban and surprised him with a rib-cracking hug. "Thank you! And who's this young man? Looks like he's related to you." She hugged Thane too. "Thank you for bringing her home!"

"She's the one who protected us." Corban gestured to Nikki's waist. "Or we never would've escaped."

Jing gawked at Nikki's sword. "Where did you get that?"

Thane spoke up. "Long story. We have a lot to tell you. I'm Thane Abrams, by the way. Corban and I are banished from West Fort."

"Eat first." Eliana was in the kitchen, pulling food out of the refrigerator. "Talk later. Mom, it looks like Nikki and Thane need your magic touch."

"Corban too." Nikki glanced sideways at his neck.

Jing took a closer look. "Darkness! It looks like someone tried to strangle you!"

"Someone did." Nikki slipped off her shoes and sank into the nearest chair. "Their uncle, the mayor, tied me up and kept me prisoner in the kitchen cellar until Corban found me." She turned to Derek in the other chair with Travis asleep in his arms. "Thank you for sending him the message. If he'd come five minutes later, it would've been too late. I would've been sent outside the fort."

"Darkness." The color drained from Solona's face. She ushered Thane and Corban over to the couch. "Sit down. Let me get my kit."

"We looked a lot worse before Ms. Vaughn took us in." Thane sat still for Solona's ministrations. He winced as she rubbed healing oils on his swollen, bruised, and misshapen nose.

Jing went to the kitchen to assist Eliana with scrambled eggs and toast.

"Who's Ms. Vaughn?" Derek asked.

"Wait a minute," Nikki said. "We need to start from the beginning."

"Please do." Derek covered a huge yawn. *We're relieved you're back safe,* he added.

Nikki described what happened to her from the time she left the library until the time they walked in the door, with Corban or Thane interrupting a few times to add clarifying details.

Eliana dished up seven plates of eggs and toast, and Jing helped her distribute them around the sitting room. The only sounds for the next few minutes were forks scraping plates.

Solona broke the silence with a thoughtful question. "So we know Leighton Abrams is supervising the secret construction on Seventh Fort, but why?"

"The fort is part of the puzzle," Corban said. "We suspect he's also hidden a stockpile of weapons."

Solona's eyes widened. "Weapons? You're sure?"

"I found them by accident," Corban said. "Mostly rifles but a few handguns."

"Do we know he hid them?" Solona looked worried. "We can't accuse him without proof."

"I heard him discussing it with another man, in his memories." Nikki flinched as all eyes shifted to her. "He said they convinced the hunters to donate their rifles."

"But rifles are useless if there's no bullets," Thane said, "which is why the guild stopped using rifles in the first place."

120

"According to the other man, they have a way to make more." Nikki stared at her empty plate. "Abrams let go of me before I heard anything else."

"Reloading press," Corban spoke up.

Thane grimaced. "I forgot about that."

"What is it?" Solona asked.

"It's a machine used to make new bullets from empty cartridges," Thane said. "The Hunters Guild master has one. Before the guild stopped using guns, we were required to turn over our used cartridges to him after each hunt."

"So there's a way to produce more ammo?" Nikki asked.

"Until they run out of gunpowder and primers, yes," Thane said. "I don't know how much they managed to produce."

"The colony's run out of everything we can't make ourselves," Derek said. "Once engines wear out, we'll have no more transportation—the few trucks still running have the last of the replacement parts inside."

Thane nodded in agreement. "The one I drove to Seventh Fort a few days ago was at the end of its life."

"About the guns—my brother Zhao could tell us who stockpiled them," Jing said.

Everyone turned to look at her with raised eyebrows. "He's like Nikki, only with inanimate objects."

Her explanation brought nods of agreement.

"Derek, please send him a message," Solona said. "Ask Zhao Kaczenski to come here and speak to me in person. Which guild is he in, Jing?"

"Mechanics."

"That means he goes to Waterfall. Derek, contact him now, before he goes to work. Corban, could you tell him how to find the cache?"

"I can show him," Corban said.

"No." Solona's tone was firm. "You and Thane need to go into hiding."

"But where can we—?" Thane said.

"Here?" Nikki didn't mean to sound eager, but she noted her mother's raised eyebrows and Corban's flushed face and corrected herself. "Bad idea?"

"This is the first place he'll look," Solona said. "You'll be safer at Jing's. Corban and Thane could stay with Eliana and Derek."

"You know we'd love to help, Mom, but a new baby makes it hard to get much sleep," Eliana said.

"We don't want to impose," Thane said. "We've already imposed enough on your hospitality."

Solona turned to him with a fierce expression. "You saved my daughter's life. You're part of our family now."

Corban and Thane exchanged stunned expressions.

"One of the ships?" Eliana said. "No one uses them except during the storm."

"The library?" Nikki studied the brothers' faces for a reaction. "We'd set you up with food, bedding, whatever you need."

"Uncle wouldn't expect to find Corban in the library." Thane's remark brought a few chuckles to the room.

"Contact Zhao." Solona nodded to Derek. Her gaze swept Nikki, Corban, and Thane. "I know you three are exhausted, but we need to hide you before Leighton or his thugs come looking. Nikki, pack a bag and go with Jing."

"Yes, ma'am." Nikki headed to the bedroom she shared with her mother. Jing followed her and shut the door.

"Your father lets you stay here anytime, but I've never stayed at your place. Do you think he'll mind?" Nikki pulled a duffle bag out of the wardrobe and tossed some clothes into it.

"Yes, but we'll tell him your mom's sick. He's paranoid of germs. Besides, he thinks you're Normal."

Nikki gaped at her. "You lied to him?"

"He'd never let me be friends with you if he knew you're a Stray."

***

In their rush to leave, Nikki didn't get a chance to say goodbye to Thane and Corban, but she suspected she would see more of them, especially if they were hiding in the library. She and Jing made their way down the second-floor hallway to the Kaczenski apartment in the east wall.

Zhao and Kun had already left for work, so Jing let Nikki have her bed and she took Zhao's in the larger bedroom he shared with Kun. They both slept until early afternoon.

Nikki woke to the smell of grilled cheese sandwiches. She followed the scent into the kitchen.

"How crispy do you like yours?" Jing was standing over a frying pan at the tiny two-burner stove.

"I like it just shy of burnt." Nikki found a pitcher of apple juice in the refrigerator. "Does it feel like we're organizing some type of resistance?"

"We are." Jing tipped two sandwiches onto waiting plates. "A secret fort and a stockpile of guns are good reasons to think about a defensive strategy."

Nikki leaned her elbows on the counter and bit a corner off her steaming grilled cheese. "Who are we defending ourselves from?"

"Survivors, I guess. Slime worms like Leighton Abrams and others who have his attitude toward Strays."

"You're sure?"

"You tell me. You said Leighton grabbed you several times yesterday. What did you see in his memories?"

Nikki took her time pouring two glasses of juice to avoid looking Jing in the eye. "I don't know if I should tell you. At least, not until I talk to Corban since he was in most of them. How soon do you think Zhao can investigate the cache?"

"You're changing the subject."

"Yes, I am." Nikki's frown morphed into a scowl. "We need to know what we're up against, how many people are in on Abrams's plan."

Jing's face fell. "Like *Baba?*"

"No." Nikki tried to sound reassuring, but Jing didn't appear convinced. "He might be afraid of Strays, but your dad's not a violent man."

Jing wiped away a tear from the corner of her eye. "He said he'd send Zhao outside the fort like a criminal. He wants to banish his own son. He's never hit either of us, but I don't know what he's capable of. He's interested in Abrams's twisted views." She rubbed her other eye, her expression turning fierce. "If I have to choose sides, you know I'll stand with you and Zhao."

Nikki opened her mouth to respond, but Derek's voice interrupted her thoughts. *Zhao is going to check out the stockpile during lunch and wants Jing to keep a lookout. He'll meet her at the weird tree.* She repeated the message aloud.

Jing nodded. "I'll take my bike."

***

Nikki didn't want Kun Kaczenski to catch her alone in their apartment, so she hid in Jing's room while she waited for her friend to return. She had known the Kaczenskis for most of her life, but being around the guild master always made her uncomfortable. He was an opinionated and unpleasant man who hadn't gotten over his wife's death from the Plague. Nikki hated the way Kun criticized Zhao and sometimes Jing. She thought about Corban and Thane's home life, and realized how fortunate she was to have one good parent.

She found two extra blankets and a pillow in Jing's wardrobe and set up a place to sleep on the floor between Jing's bed and the wall so no one could see it from the doorway. She shoved her duffle bag and sword under the bed and lay down on her make-shift nest to wait.

Nikki pondered Brida Vaughn's strange advice about choosing the memories she wanted to see. *How can I do that? Seems like I'd need to practice, but who would be willing to let me see all their memories?*

"Nikki?" Jing poked her head in the doorway.

She sat up from behind the bed. "Over here." She was surprised to see both Jing and Zhao step inside the room. "What happened? Doesn't Zhao need to go back to work?"

Jing's face was pale. "We need to tell you something."

"What?" Nikki drew her knees up to her chin and wrapped her arms around her legs.

Zhao perched on the foot of his sister's bed next to Nikki. His skin was medium-dark and his eyes were narrow like Jing's, but his black hair was buzzed short. It refused to lie flat, sticking straight up around his scalp. Zhao rubbed at the threadbare knees of his blue work coveralls and took his time explaining. "*Baba*'s hands were all over those guns, along with Leighton Abrams, East Fort's mayor Mariposa Savoy, and several guild masters . . . including Elian Ramirez."

Nikki felt as if the air was being squeezed from her lungs. "Why does the Farmers Guild master care about collecting guns? And for what purpose?"

"You tell us." Jing shifted from one foot to the other. "Didn't you say he wanted nothing to do with you and Eliana because you're Strays?"

"I haven't seen my father since Mom threw him out of the apartment. I have no idea what he's been up to the past ten storms." Her stomach turned queasy. "All I know is he lives in Greenfield, remarried a long time ago, and recently became guild master."

"I guess he's been spending time with Leighton Abrams." Zhao turned to Jing. "I'm not safe here anymore. If *Baba*'s involved with whatever's going on, I need to go into hiding with Thane and Corban."

"If your dad finds out I'm a Stray—" Nikki felt a flutter of panic. "I can't stay here either."

"He doesn't know," Jing said.

126

"Not until he talks to his pal Abrams." Zhao stood. "I need to pack and leave before *Baba* gets home."

Jing was angry. "No, you've done nothing wrong. Why should you have to hide from *Baba*?" She scrutinized Nikki's expression. "What do either of you have to be afraid of?"

"I'm on West Fort's most wanted list," Nikki said. "I'm not even sure if I'm safe showing my face around Lakeside."

"Mayor Brooks will protect you—both of you," Jing said. "Let's consider other options before you go into hiding. Why don't we go talk to her?"

"Maybe we should leave it to Solona," Zhao said. "She has some leverage among the colony leaders." He turned to leave the room. "You can do what you want, but I'd feel safer leaving now."

Nikki didn't know what to do. "I'm scared."

"Please stay," Jing said. "*Baba* doesn't know you're a Stray, and he rarely goes to West Fort. You'll be safe here, for now."

"I don't know."

"Stay in my room when he's home. If we're careful, he won't even know you're here."

"It's a small apartment." Nikki frowned. "He's going to notice."

"Let's try it for now." Jing was pleading. "I'll go talk to your mom, tell her to meet with Mayor Brooks."

Nikki knew her friend was as scared as she was. "Both our fathers are involved in this—whatever it is. Are you prepared to run away from home, like Zhao, if something bad happens?"

Jing nodded. "Let's hope something bad doesn't happen. We have to stay a step ahead of Abrams. Whatever he's planning is going to send the colony into civil war if we don't do something to stop him."

"I agree." Zhao was back, standing in the doorway. He was wearing a backpack stuffed to capacity. He stepped over to Jing and kissed her on the cheek. "Be careful not to come to the library too often, in case someone's watching the landing strip."

Nikki blew out a long breath. "Aren't you being paranoid?"

"No, just cautious." Zhao nodded to Nikki and left the apartment.

THIRTEEN
NEW ROOMMATE

Thane woke to the sounds of footsteps on the ladder. "Corban!" He sat up and looked around the tiny cone-shaped room.

"Whazz?" Corban muttered, half-asleep with the blanket over his head.

The highest level of the library ship was illuminated by two round port windows, but Thane didn't have a clue what time of day it was. He struggled to get up from his bedroll on the floor. "Someone's coming up the ladder." He raised his voice, but Corban didn't move.

No one knows we're here except the people in Solona's apartment this morning. Thane wrestled with his apprehension as he limped over to the ladder and peered over the edge of the hole.

A young man whose features resembled Jing's spotted him from several levels below. "Are you all the way up on the bridge?"

"Not the bridge anymore," Thane said. "It's stripped bare. Are you Zhao?"

"Yes." Zhao didn't ask anything else as he focused on finishing the climb to level fifteen. He stepped off the ladder, breathing hard, and offered Thane his hand.

"We thought it'd be safer camping far away from the library level. I'm Thane." He shook the younger man's hand, which was as callused as his own.

"Nice to meet you. Hope you don't mind if I go into hiding with you and your brother." Zhao studied the yawning lump on the floor that was Corban. He shrugged off his backpack and set it by his feet.

"Last I heard before we left Solona's, you were going to investigate the weapons stockpile. Did something happen? Did you get caught?"

"No, but my father's hands were all over those guns, along with your uncle's."

Thane grimaced. "Anyone else?"

Zhao nodded, his expression grim. "I wrote a list for Solona. I detected several guild masters and colony leaders, including Nikki's father."

"Darkness." Thane limped back over to his bedroll. "Make yourself at home." He sat on the floor and dug his brace out of his backpack.

Corban sat up and blinked sleepily at Zhao. "Did you bring anything to eat?"

Zhao sat on the floor between their bedrolls and opened his pack. "I stopped by the dining hall before coming here. Solona said they'll arrange a drop-off point to leave food for us every day." He took out three chicken salad sandwiches and handed the brothers their portions. A bottle of orange juice with three ceramic cups was unearthed, along with a bag of carrot sticks and cucumber slices.

"Healthy food." Thane feigned a sigh.

"Who cares?" Corban said around a mouthful of sandwich. "I'm hungry."

"Nice to meet you, Corban." Zhao shot him a bemused grin and continued recounting his tale. "My old man's been threatening me for a while so I thought I'd be safer leaving. If he knew Nikki's a Stray, I wouldn't let her stay in our apartment, but Jing thinks she'll be safe for now."

"He doesn't know?" Corban asked, surprised. "Hasn't she been friends with Jing for a long time?"

Zhao said, "Jing told me Solona doesn't want anyone to know about her Talent."

"It's hard to hide being a Stray if you're our age," Thane said. "Half the people I grew up with are Strays."

Corban swallowed a huge bite of sandwich. "I think Solona's trying to do more than shield her from bigots. Nikki has a Talent that could be a threat to whatever Uncle's planning."

Zhao munched a carrot stick. "Maybe if Nikki could focus on specific memories, but Jing told me she can't. She gets all of them, and in no particular order. It took me a long time to learn to focus my Talent. I used to be the same way."

"Could you demonstrate for us?" Thane asked.

"Sure." Zhao leaned over and placed his hand on Corban's *Bushcraft: Outdoor Survival Guide* on the floor next to his pillow. "I'm getting half a dozen impressions, but I have to concentrate to put them in chronological order." He shut his eyes. "This is Corban's but Thane's touched it too. I can tell it was your father Harrison's and your grandfather Nathaniel's, but those impressions are faint."

Thane experienced a pang of sadness, but his burning curiosity shoved it aside. "Anyone else?"

"It was handled briefly by Cassidy, Thessa, and Nia Abrams, your mother, grandmother, and great-grandmother. This is very old. It first belonged to Devon Abrams, your great-grandfather."

Corban's astonished exhale sounded like a leaky balloon.

"His mother, Leigh Abrams, gave it to him, probably as a gift. After it was printed, it was handled by someone who boxed it up for shipping. Her name was Ling, Mei Lin. It was placed on a store shelf by Vicki Davis and touched by a cashier named Tony Braden before Leigh gave it to Devon."

Thane was speechless.

Zhao opened his eyes and took his hand off the book. "Before I learned to control my Talent, I'd get a flood of names in my mind. I learned to focus on them one at a time and determine which one was the strongest."

"Strongest?" Corban asked.

"I get stronger impressions from the most recent contact or the person who touched the item longer than anyone else." Zhao nodded toward the *Bushcraft* book. "That's been in your possession the longest, but your great-grandfather handled it more than anyone."

"Do you get these impressions every time you touch something?" Thane asked.

"Fortunately, no. I can tune it out for my daily activities."

"Yes, I guess it'd be a headache to know the names of everyone who climbed the ladder," Corban said.

"Worse, everyone who picked up the spoon I used in the dining hall." Zhao nodded. "I learned to control my Talent because it has the potential to make me insane. I think Nikki needs to practice with hers to gain the same level of control. She has to be able to choose which memories she wants to see."

"That's what Brida said." Thane nodded to Corban.

"Who's Brida?" Zhao asked.

"Long story." Thane refilled his cup with orange juice. "What else can you tell us about the guns?"

"I'm not worried about your uncle staging a coup right away, "Zhao said. "Not when there's no bullets."

"Why bother to stockpile guns with no ammunition?" Corban asked.

"I'm guessing they stashed the ammo somewhere else," Zhao said, "in case someone found the guns."

"Where?" Thane asked.

"No idea." Zhao bit into his sandwich.

"I think the Hunters Guild master still has the reloading press. Maybe he's storing the bullets." Corban brushed the crumbs from his hands.

"He lives in Orchard Valley," Thane said. "Seems pointless to store the ammo so far away from the guns."

"We could speculate about it all day." Corban eyed his brother. "What we need is more information. Since we're in hiding, Uncle might talk more freely about what he's got planned."

"I'd have to find a secluded spot near the fort to eavesdrop. But he's at Seventh during the day."

"He's not always at Seventh," Corban said. "He caught Nikki yesterday."

Thane frowned. "Has it only been a day?" He touched the bridge of his nose and winced at the fresh stab of pain. "Yes," he answered his own question.

"Which reminds me." Zhao rummaged in one of his backpack's outer pockets and found a small brown bottle. "Solona wants you to apply a few drops to your nose twice a day. She said to rub a tiny bit under your eyes to clear up the bruises, but be careful not to get it in your eyes. She said Corban should also use it on his neck."

Thane accepted the bottle with a nod of thanks. "I'll find a stakeout spot tomorrow. Maybe I'll hear something useful."

***

Before his encounter with the night terror, Thane had been a decent hunter, but now it was difficult to traverse the woods with his limp. He left the ship right after dawn and avoided the roads, cutting through the dense trees toward West Fort. It took him twice as long to cover ground as people with two normal legs, so he resigned himself to a long day outside. He didn't mind, as long as he didn't get Ilios-burned like Rupert.

He found a fallen tree within sight of the battlements and sat on it. The space was surrounded by saplings covered with enough new leaves to hide him from prying eyes, he hoped. Thane knew he might eavesdrop all day and not hear anything useful, but he was determined to do his part to find out what his uncle was planning. He had a machete, in case he encountered a bluedeer, plus a water bottle and a few apples. Inadequate supplies for a long stakeout, but it couldn't be helped, not until Solona sent more food to the ship.

Leighton's voice was the easiest to identify amidst the murmur of dozens of random conversations, but Thane didn't hear him. *He probably went to Seventh Fort this morning.* He scanned the audio babble for another familiar voice and was able to hone in on Chaim Rajamani's. The guild master was talking to a woman Thane didn't recognize.

"Relax, Mari. You didn't have to come all the way to West Fort today. Leighton is planning to meet with all the mayors soon."

"I'm not the one who needs to relax." Her tone was scornful. "Kun told me Leighton barged in on Lake-side's community council meeting last week. He's already raised Brooks's suspicions. All this work will be for nothing if the vote's not unanimous."

"It'll be fine," Chaim said. "Pavitra will do as she's told."

"She has three grown children who are Strays," the woman called Mari said. "Don't underestimate her."

"Don't assume parents of Strays are going to resist the plan. Most of them think like you and Kun— eager to have them out of the way."

"Aren't you concerned Leighton's nephews and Kun's son have vanished? They could be anywhere, planning a resistance."

That's exactly what we're doing, Thane thought.

Chaim snorted. "Am I worried about three worthless Strays disappearing? Thane's so weak, I wouldn't be surprised if a pack of night terrors took care of him already."

Thane snapped a branch off the tree he was sitting on. He made an effort to suppress his emotions so he didn't lose focus.

"Keep your voice down," Mari said.

Chaim laughed. "You think my apprentices can hear anything while they're pounding anvils? Conquist's probably stone deaf by now."

Mari didn't sound so confident. "None of them are Strays?"

"All Normals," Chaim said. "It's nice not having a worthless Stray in the shed, spying on my conversations."

"Spying?"

"Thane Abrams can hear things. I don't trust him, and neither does his uncle."

"My daughter can make things move," Mari said. "It's always bothered me. It's like living with a ghost. It was a relief when she moved into the Tanners Guild. Maybe they'll find some use for her."

"I doubt it," Chaim said. "She'll be put to better use living with the other Strays."

"I still don't see how you're going to convince them to leave."

Chaim's chuckle was anything but cheerful. "Don't worry, Abrams's plan will work."

"I hope you're right. You could ignite a civil war if you're wrong."

"It won't come to that." The arrogance in Chaim's tone made Thane see red. He found another branch and snapped it in two, imagining for a moment it was Rajamani's neck.

Convince the Strays to leave? Are they planning to force us out at gunpoint? Thane was certain he had stumbled on the real plan.

FOURTEEN
NEW ALLY

Nikki wanted to go to school, but she didn't want to risk being caught by one of Abrams's soldiers, so she spent the next several days hiding out in Jing's room, reading her friend's small collection of books she had read twice before, and worrying about what was going on in the colony. Kun Kaczenski rarely checked on his daughter to see how she was doing. He sounded happy to have Zhao gone, that much was clear from conversations Nikki overheard between him and Jing. He was often absent, returning to the apartment late in the evening and leaving again early the next morning.

"He hasn't said a word about Corban's uncle," Jing told her after school on fourth-day. "Here, I brought you a sandwich."

Nikki was tired of sandwiches and whatever fruits and vegetables Jing brought from the dining hall. She wanted to sit down to a decent meal, but she was more concerned about how Corban, Thane, and Zhao were coping. "Let's go to the library today."

Jing frowned. "I told Mr. Gupta you were sick."

"He won't see me. I've got to get out of this apartment before I go crazy. I feel like a prisoner." She studied her friend's expression. "Is anyone even looking for me? Have you spoken to any sentries?"

"No." Jing shrugged.

"Then we don't know if Abrams has a warrant out for my arrest." Nikki stood and stretched. "No offense, but your room is boring."

Jing furrowed her brow. "Are you sure it's safe for you to leave the fort?"

"No, but let's find out." Nikki pulled on her bluedeer-skin boots. "Come on."

She led the way with Jing trailing two steps behind. When they reached the bottom of the stairs that exited onto the street, Nikki spoke over her shoulder. "Try to relax. We don't want to attract attention."

Jing caught up and they stepped outside the building together.

"The sentry will wonder why you look constipated," Nikki whispered. "Act natural."

"I'm trying." Jing smoothed out her furrowed brow.

When they reached the archway, Nikki turned her face away from the sentry, who was stationed by one of the tall doors, and pretended to be deep in conversation with Jing. "I think I did well on my advanced math test. What did you make?"

"I'm not taking advanced math." Jing's high-pitched reply earned a scowl from Nikki.

They had almost slipped past the guard when he showed a sudden interest in them. "Are you Nikolasa Ramirez?"

Nikki tried to think fast. "No, she's one of my classmates. Why do you ask?" She turned to face the middle-aged man with what she hoped was an innocent smile.

"You match her description." The sentry took a step toward them, his mouth set in a thin line.

Jing panicked and ran, leaving Nikki no choice but to do the same. They raced down the path toward the lake, leaving the sentry behind.

"Wait!" the guard shouted. "Mayor Brooks wants to talk to you!"

Nikki hesitated, staring at Jing's retreating back. "Maybe we should hear what she has to say!"

Jing skidded to a stop and peered at Nikki over her shoulder. "Are you crazy? She'll lock you up."

"Why would she do that?" Nikki turned and faced the sentry, who caught up to her in a few strides. "Why does the mayor want to see me?"

The heavy guard frowned, wheezing a little from the unexpected exercise. The name on his tag said *T. Bjoeren*. "You'll have to ask her. Come with me." He reached out to take Nikki's arm.

"No, don't touch me." She evaded his grasp. "I'll follow you."

Jing trotted back to join them. "May I go with her?"

Bjoeren shrugged and turned back toward the fort. The two young women grimaced at each other behind his back as they followed him to the gates.

"This can't be good." Jing's whisper was barely audible. "What if Brooks turns you over to Abrams?"

Nikki shook her head, refusing to give voice to her fear. When they were back inside the entrance to the fort, she told Bjoeren, "Since I'm a minor, my mother should be present when I speak to Mayor Brooks. Do you mind if my friend goes to get her?"

The sentry shrugged again, his disgruntled expression unchanged.

"She'll be at the apartment or the apothecary in the marketplace," she told Jing.

Jing rolled her eyes at Nikki before heading toward the Zegarelli apartment.

"This way." Bjoeren opened the door to the south wall staircase and led her up to the third floor. He pounded on door number 34S.

"Enter!" a woman's voice rang out.

Bjoeren opened the door and waited for Nikki to slip by him at the threshold. "Nikolasa Ramirez, as requested." He pulled the door shut behind her.

Pavitra Brooks looked up from a simple table she was using as a desk in the middle of the room. "Come in, Ms. Ramirez. I promise you're not in trouble." She was a short, plump, dark-skinned woman with straight, waist-length black hair, streaked with a fair amount of gray, and an unusual red dot painted in the middle of her forehead. The mayor stood and gestured for Nikki to take one of the chairs in front of the desk.

"My mother's coming." Nikki settled into a hard wooden seat.

"Good!" Mayor Brooks flashed a gap-toothed smile and settled back in her own chair. "I've tried to corner Solona for days now. Shrewd woman, your mother. It wouldn't surprise me if she ran for mayor next election."

"Mom hates politics," Nikki said.

"I do too. I was hoping my opponent would win, especially after I learned what kind of slime worms I'd have to deal with in East and West Forts." Brooks leaned back in her seat, the wooden joints squeaking in protest. "While we're waiting, tell me about your encounter with Leighton Abrams. I've heard several versions of the story, each more outrageous than the last."

"I wouldn't call it an encounter. More like an assault." Nikki shifted in her chair. "Although I may have provoked him by snooping in his apartment." She went on to explain the details of her capture, imprisonment, and escape, although she was careful not to mention who aided her in sneaking out of West Fort.

"He tied you up and left you in a cellar?" Mayor Brooks was outraged. "And he was going to evict you from the fort during the night?"

"Yes, ma'am."

"Breaking and entering isn't a crime punishable by death. You did nothing to provoke such abuse."

"Just being a Stray is a crime, in Abrams's opinion," Nikki said. "He's a violent man. The way he abused his nephews, since they were babies, was horrible."

Before Brooks replied, there was a sharp knock at the door.

"I assume that's Solona," the mayor said. "Come in!"

Nikki was relieved to see her mother poke her head inside the room. "Hello, Pavitra. Do you mind if Jing Kaczenski joins us?"

"Come on in. We'll have a party." Mayor Brooks stood to greet the newcomers. "Pull up a chair."

Nikki shot a nervous eye-roll at Jing as her friend slid into the seat at her left. Solona gave her daughter a curious look before sitting on her right.

"Something stinks like a night terror, and the odor leads straight to Leighton Abrams." Brooks dropped back into her chair.

"I agree," Solona said.

"What shall we do about it?" the mayor said.

"I'm not sure what we can do," Solona said, "since we don't know exactly what he has planned."

"Venture a guess." Brooks's eyes swiveled to Nikki. "What do you think is going on?"

Nikki thought back to the memories she glimpsed in Abrams's mind. "He said the Strays won't go willingly."

"Go where?" Brooks frowned.

"Seventh Fort," Nikki said.

"Seventh Fort is still in the planning stages," the mayor said.

Nikki shook her head. "Thane Abrams saw it a few days ago. He said the exterior's finished."

Brooks turned to Solona. "Is this true?"

"I haven't seen it myself, but I trust Thane's word. Tell her about the guns."

The mayor gasped. "Guns?"

Jing spoke up. "I went with my brother to check out the stockpile a few days ago. Corban Abrams discovered it by accident in the woods near West Fort. I kept watch on the road while Zhao climbed down in the hole to take a closer look. Leighton Abrams's hands were all over them. So were my father's."

"My ex-husband's too." Solona scowled.

"How do you know?" Brooks's cheeks were almost as red as the dot on her forehead.

"Zhao can identify who touched any object," Jing said. "It's his Talent."

"The slime worm is planning a coup!" The mayor got to her feet and paced behind her desk. "He's been plotting this right under our noses!"

"It would seem that way," Solona said.

"What can we do to stop him?" Brooks paced faster, her face screwed up in concentration. "The first thing we should do is empty the cache. He can't threaten Strays if he doesn't have guns."

"There's no ammunition," Jing said. "The slime worm already thought of that in case someone found the cache. We think he hid the ammo somewhere else."

"Even if we took the guns, we can't defend ourselves with them without the ammo. What we need to do is organize the Strays," Nikki said.

Her mother's shoulders slumped. "The colony is spread out between the six forts, and we have no way to communicate anymore except through messengers."

"Derek could send messages to anyone," Nikki said, "and Rupert Conquist, Thane's friend. I'm sure other Strays have the Talent for sending messages."

"But how to locate them?" Jing asked. "Most Strays are like you, Nik. They keep quiet about their Talents to avoid harassment."

"Not everyone hates Strays." Nikki set her jaw. "We can't allow Abrams to force us all to live in Seventh Fort. If it is a fort."

Brooks stopped in her tracks and gave Nikki a startled look. "What do you mean?"

"I mean I saw the blueprints, and Thane saw it with his own eyes. Seventh has no exterior windows. What if Abrams intends to use it as a prison?"

"Japanese internment camps," Brooks muttered under her breath.

"Warsaw Ghetto." Solona nodded in agreement.

"Sorry, what are you talking about?" Nikki asked.

"Second World War, Earth history," Brooks said. "These were places designed to keep people of a certain race or religion confined."

"Under armed guard," Solona said.

"I'm not going!" Nikki was on her feet. "And I'm not waiting around for the forced roundup of Strays—if that's what he's planning. What can we do to stop him?"

"I don't know," Solona said. "We'll need a plan of our own."

Mayor Brooks stared out the window, her brow furrowed. "I know two of the mayors are anti-Stray, but I'm not sure about the other three. I'll see what I can do to organize Lakeside, at least. I'll ask Pastor Martin to speak to the congregation on seventh-day, and arrange a meeting with our guild masters as soon as possible."

"No need to invite my father." Jing's tone was bitter.

Brooks gave her a sympathetic look. "I know, but don't give up on him yet. You might be the leverage we need to persuade him to see reason."

Solona got to her feet. "Let's get busy. We need to spread the word to as many people as we can. Thank you, Pavitra, for your help."

"I have three children who are Strays," the mayor said, "and there's no way in darkness I'm going to let a slime worm like Leighton Abrams lock them up."

FIFTEEN
MAYORS COUNCIL

"They're meeting tonight," Jing announced the moment she stepped off the ladder.

Thane was glad to see her but kept his expression as serious as Nikki's, Corban's, and Zhao's, who were seated around the table with him.

Jing slid into the open chair next to Zhao. "They chose a central location—Waterfall. *Baba* said he wouldn't be home before dark and that Mayor DeKalb is putting him up in a guest room for the night."

Corban turned to Thane. "You have to listen to every word."

"I have to be inside the fort to eavesdrop on a night meeting. You know I won't make it past the sentries."

"You're assuming the sentries will be looking for you, but I don't think that's the case," Jing said. "An issue affecting West Fort doesn't affect the others."

"How can you be sure?" Thane studied her round face, grateful for an excuse to do so.

"When was the last time you heard news from the other forts since the satellite went offline?" Jing asked.

"It's true. The only news we get is gossip," Nikki said.

"But you don't know Uncle," Thane said. "The man's relentless. He'll have wanted posters up for us in every fort."

"I haven't seen posters in Lakeside," Jing said. "And you know Nikki would be recognized there. Are you sure you're not being paranoid?"

"You've met him, right?" Corban raised an eyebrow at Nikki. "You think he's going to let it go?"

"Met him?" Nikki scowled. "If I had a choice between him and a night terror, I'd pick the night terror."

"We could disguise you," Jing said.

Thane shook his head. "My limp's difficult to hide. And what about my black eyes?

"I've seen several old men with limps in the colony," Nikki said. "If we gave you gray hair, dark glasses, and a cane, I think you'd pass the Waterfall sentries undetected."

Thane was uneasy about the plan but knew their options were limited. He needed to eavesdrop on the meeting. "If you think a disguise will work, let's do it. It's getting late."

Nikki got to her feet. "Come on, Jing, I think we can find what we need in the hospital. We'll be right back." The two young women hurried to the ladder and descended out of sight.

Corban, Thane, and Zhao sat in thoughtful silence until Nikki and Jing returned twenty minutes later, each with a cloth bundle under one arm. They spread the pilfered items on the table.

"How did you sneak this past the nurse?" Thane picked up a brown bottle of hydrogen peroxide from the pile. "Won't this turn my hair white?"

"You could shave your head later," Jing said.

Thane frowned but held off grumbling. He liked his long hair and preferred its natural blond color.

"Jing convinced the nurse she had stomach pain. I rifled through lockers while they were in the exam room." Nikki held up a pair of dark glasses with scratched lenses. "Patients have been leaving stuff in the ship for a long time."

"I know *mei mei*'s a good actress." Zhao unfolded the white cane for a visually impaired person. "But how did you convince the nurse you were cured so you could leave?"

"All I did was burp." Jing shrugged.

Nikki snorted. "She rattled off a belch louder than a night terror's growl and said, 'I feel better now, thanks.'"

"Nikki!" Jing's face turned pink as the others howled with laughter.

Thane was quick to change the subject. "I'll need a scribe to write down what I hear at the meeting."

"I'll do it." Jing scowled. "I want to hear what my father has to say."

A part of Thane looked forward to spending time with her, even though the circumstances were serious. "Thank you." He stood with the bottle of peroxide in hand. "Let's get this over with. Kitchen sink?"

Nikki pulled an old towel and a pair of latex gloves from the pile. "I'll help."

An hour later, Thane was transformed into an elderly man with white hair and beard, dark glasses, baggy jacket and pants to hide his brace, and a walking cane. The smell of peroxide was stuck in his nostrils.

"Excellent," Corban said. "If I can't recognize you, you should be safe from Uncle."

"You can ride on the handlebars of my bike until we get close to Waterfall," Jing said. "Then we'll hide the bike and I'll walk you through the gates. You should lean on my arm like you can't see."

Thane nodded. He was looking forward to leaning on Jing, if only for a few minutes.

Nikki said, "Jing, you can stay in the Herbalists Guild's barracks tonight. You've been there before with me. It's on the second floor of the northeast corner, number 20E. Tell them you have Solona's permission and they won't turn you away."

"I hope Rupert can find a place to hide me overnight," Thane said. "Let's all meet back here in the morning."

Jing leaned over to offer Zhao a peck on the cheek. "See you tomorrow."

"Be safe, *mei mei.*"

"Good luck." Corban's words to his brother were sincere. "Have Rupert keep us informed."

***

Thane didn't need to worry about being identified by the Waterfall sentries. The two uniformed women at the gates didn't give him a second look. "Did I ruin my hair for nothing?" he murmured in Jing's ear.

"Shhh. Let's find Rupert."

Rupert found them before they wandered far from the gate. "There you are." He came up on Thane's other side and took his free arm. "We've been searching for you everywhere, Grandpa."

"Be quiet." Thane ignored his friend's laughter. "Get me indoors so I can listen."

"Keep your dentures in, I've got it covered." Rupert led the way to the north wall and upstairs to a third floor apartment, number 33N. He knocked and it was answered by a former classmate Thane recognized.

Robin Aziz was in the Hunters Guild, but from the looks of her bulging belly, she wasn't tracking bluedeer anymore. She ushered them into the apartment and shut the door before speaking.

"Thane, nice to see you. You look—different. Rupert's told us all about Seventh Fort. Angus, my husband, is a Stray. We're willing to do whatever we can to help." She placed a hand on her baby bump. "For her sake, as well as ours."

"Thank you." Thane shed the glasses so he was able to see clearer. "And congratulations."

Robin beamed. "Thanks. We're thinking of naming her Solona."

"Good choice," Thane said. "How did you manage to get an apartment so fast?"

Robin's smile vanished. "We didn't. We live with Angus's mother. She's a sentry and on duty tonight or we couldn't have pulled this off."

Thane grinned. "I think we walked past her to get here."

"We told her she needs to decide whose side she's on," Robin said. "Things are going to get ugly for us and her future granddaughter if she listens to your uncle."

Thane thought of the gun cache. "I just hope we can prevent any bloodshed."

Robin bit her lip and nodded.

Jing broke the silence. "I'm Jing Kaczenski." She stuck out her hand to shake Robin's. "Nice to meet you. Do you have a quiet room Thane could use for eavesdropping?"

"Of course. My bedroom's right over here."

Jing eyed Thane with apprehension before heading toward the door Robin indicated. Thane shut the door after Rupert, grateful Robin didn't want to join them since he was nervous enough. He sat on the foot of the bed, and Jing sat on the floor with her legs crossed. She dug a folded sheet of paper and a pen out of her cargo pocket.

Rupert leaned over the wooden cradle pushed up against the open window and peered outside between the drawn curtains. "Have they started, Stumpy?"

Thane put a finger to his lips, cautioning his friend not to break his concentration. He shut his eyes and tuned his ears, seeking out a familiar voice amidst the babble of hundreds of conversations. It took a moment to hone in on Leighton, who was already addressing the meeting of the colony's mayors. Without preamble, Thane repeated what he heard.

"'I'm glad you're all here tonight'—Leighton's speaking—'and I want to thank you for being willing to meet with me.'

"'This better be good'—a woman's voice."

"Probably Lakeside's mayor, Pavitra Brooks," Jing whispered. Her pen flew across the page without a pause. "She's on our side."

"'I think we should discuss what to do about the Strays.'

"'They're adults now'—not sure who's speaking, a man—'and their contributions to the colony are essential, in my opinion. What's there to discuss?'

"'Their Talents and the potential threat they pose to Survivors.'

"'What threat?'—Brooks—'What evidence do you have that they're anything but law-abiding, hard-working citizens, Leighton?'

"'They make me nervous!'—sounds like your dad, Jing.

"'Your paranoia doesn't make them a problem, Kun! If you have something to share, get on with it!'"

"I really like Mayor Brooks," Rupert whispered.

"'My son is strange,'—Kun's speaking—'he knows things about objects. He can pick up a spoon and tell you who forged it. It's unnatural!'"

Thane heard Jing scratching harder at the paper, as if she needed friction to start a fire.

"'I don't see how it makes him a threat'—Brooks.

"'We've all seen how they are'—Uncle, and he sounds annoyed—'Survivors and Normals are afraid of them.'

"'As if they're somehow to blame for the changes to their DNA from the Plague?'— Brooks again—'Are the rest of you buying into this superstitious hysteria? Who else think Strays should be feared because they're different?'

"There's some muttering now." Thane tried to filter out the side conversations, but Uncle's voice cut through the din.

"'I think it's reasonable to require some limitations on their Talents—'

"'Limitations? You seem to be laboring under the delusion that our children are a problem'—Brooks—'to be controlled, somehow, to make *you* feel better.'

"'I asked you here to discuss potential problems from the unchecked use of their Talents,'—Uncle sounds mad."

"Good," Rupert said.

"'—but you won't give anyone else a chance to voice their concerns.'

"'If they have any concerns, any evidence, that Strays are somehow a danger to Survivors, I'm all ears.'

"'DeKalb, what about you?'—Uncle sounds desperate—'You told me your nephew was spying on the girls' locker room from across the street with his vision Talent.'

"'It was a long time ago,'—DeKalb sounds uncertain—'and he was only twelve. He's never done anything like it since.'

"'That you know of'—Uncle.

"'Normal behavior for a prepubescent boy, if you ask me'—Brooks.

"'No one asked you! Since you're unable to hold your tongue, would the marshal please escort Mayor Brooks from the meeting?'"

Jing snickered, turning the page over to write on the back.

"Lots of muttering now and chairs scraping the floor," Thane reported. "Door closing. Now Uncle's speaking again. 'I knew this might be controversial topic, but I'd like us all to take a minute to consider the original issue I brought up at the start of the meeting. Are the Strays a security threat to Survivors and Normals?'

"It sounds like DeKalb again. 'We know they're strange, but I'm not sure what you're implying. Do you expect the Strays to organize some sort of uprising and take over the colony?'

"'That's exactly what I think they'll do.'"

Thane winced as the volume rose, many voices shouting in either anger or agreement until Leighton called for order.

"'Let me share something that happened recently, an experience that convinces me the Strays are up to something. Five days ago, I caught a young woman from Lakeside going through my personal files in my apartment. She lied and said she was waiting to meet my nephew Corban, but when I took her arm to escort her out, she went into some sort of trance, broke free, and started shouting at me, claiming I was abusing my nephews. Then she threatened me and turned violent, and I've got the lump on my head to prove it. Why did she threaten me unless they're planning something?'"

Jing hissed and Rupert said something unrepeatable.

"'Has anyone else noticed any unusual behavior exhibited by the Strays in your communities?'

"New voice I don't recognize. 'One boy was expelled from East Fort's school for putting false thoughts into other children's minds. He convinced them to give him their valuables.'"

"Just a bully," Jing said. "There's one in every crowd. It doesn't mean all Strays are bullies."

"No, it's exactly what Leighton wants to hear," Rupert said. "It fits with his plans."

"Shhh," Thane said. "I missed what Uncle's saying. 'Since the Strays are adults now, maybe they'd feel more comfortable living together, in their own community.'"

"I knew it!" Rupert said. "He's planning to banish us."

"Lots of side discussions now," Thane said. "Leighton is shushing them. 'I know the rest of us would prefer living among our own kind. The Strays presence has created so much discord in the colony over the past sixteen storms.'"

"The only discord is in his mind, the disgusting bigot," Rupert said.

"'You're talking about segregating a large portion of the colony?'—DeKalb—'How? No one can live outside the forts. Where do you propose to move them?'

"'And what makes you think they're going to agree?'—another voice, a woman. I don't recognize her.

"'The Strays will agree to move because we've already constructed a new fort for them.'

"'What new fort?'—DeKalb—'The one being plan-ned?'

"'It's beyond planning, it's finished. The stone masons and carpenters have worked on it for months.'

"'That's impossible. How is it no one from Waterfall knew it was under construction?'—Kalb.

"'Because no one in your community was asked to work on it. West Fort houses both guilds. Construction is to the point where we can ask plumbers, electricians, and textiles to do the finishing touches.'

"'There are no more solar panels'—DeKalb sounds like he's having second thoughts—'How do you propose to run electricity to the fort?'

"'Underground cable from Waterfall.'"

"It'll never work," Rupert said. "It was tried before and abandoned because purple crawlers kept digging up the cables."

"Don't plumbers and electricians need to be involved at the beginning of a construction project?" Jing asked. "Before walls go up?"

"The fact that he's already constructed a fort for the Strays is disturbing." Rupert didn't bother to keep his voice down. "A fort with no exterior windows."

"Shhh, I need to hear what else Uncle has to say," Thane said. "He's proposing a tour for the mayors. 'Discuss this with your councils, and we'll meet again to vote on the proposal in one week. Meeting adjourned.'"

"Some proposal." Jing flexed her cramped fingers. "Abrams already put a plan in place without consulting anyone. He intends to force the Strays into exile."

"We can't let it happen," Rupert said.

"We need to get inside the fort," Jing said. "See if it really is a fort."

"What else could it be?" Rupert raised his eyebrows at her, looking confused.

"Don't be naïve," Jing said. "No plumbing or electricity? It's a prison."

SIXTEEN
IN HIDING

The orchard dream was different. The first time, during the storm, it was silent, like watching a holo-vid with no audio. This time Corban heard a voice, but it was muted, as if he was hearing Leighton's shout from the far end of a long tunnel.

"Hold it! Stop right there!"

Uncle's warning came from somewhere behind him, but the words had no effect on Nikki. She ran straight toward Corban, the expression of rage on her face identical to the one he remembered.

"Stop or I'll shoot!" Leighton's voice was muffled.

Corban was frozen in place. He couldn't look around to see where his uncle was. He wasn't able to move out of Nikki's way. She was coming right at him with the sword in her hand.

He sensed Leighton's terror, or was it his own?

"Stop!" His uncle shouted again.

She raised the sword in both hands, closed the space between them with one last stride, and swung the blade straight at Corban.

***

Corban sat up on his bedroll, clutching his neck. "Don't kill me!"

"Stop waking me up and I won't have to!" Zhao was sitting on his own bedroll, glaring over at Corban. Starlight through the port windows bathed the room in enough light for them to see each other's startled expressions.

"Sword premonition?" Thane didn't bother to sit up. "Did she cut off your head again?"

Zhao gasped. "What! Who cuts off your head?"

"Nikki." Corban rubbed his forehead, too shaken to explain.

"With the sword she gave you," Thane told Zhao, matter-of-fact, "and asked you to hide."

Zhao's gaping jaw might have been comical if Corban hadn't witnessed his own death again. "It was different this time," he told Thane. "Uncle was in it."

Thane sat up and took interest. "He was? What did you see?"

"I didn't see him. I heard him shouting, but it sounded like his voice was far away."

"He was in your dream?" Zhao was still confused.

"I don't know. Everything was the same except I heard him yelling." Corban shook his head. "He shouted, 'Stop' and 'I'll shoot.'"

"Was he yelling at you or Nikki?" Thane squinted at him.

"I don't know. I'm not even sure he was in the orchard, he sounded so far away, and why was he shouting at her to stop? Seems like he'd be happy to have her kill me."

Zhao and Thane flinched at his words.

157

Corban faced Zhao. "There's always a detail missing from my premonitions. Like the one with Nikki in the kitchen cellar. I didn't know she was down there because I woke up when I lifted the trapdoor."

"Your premonition about the tree was weird," Thane said.

"It was just a strange-looking tree." Corban nodded. "No other details. I didn't understand why I dreamt about it until I found it by accident."

Zhao frowned at Corban. "You saw your own death in a dream? Nikki's really going to chop off your head?"

"Yes." Corban slumped back onto his blanket.

"It doesn't make sense," Zhao said. "I've seen the way she looks at you, and I think she'd rather cut off her own head than do anything to hurt you."

Corban silently agreed, but Zhao's words did nothing to soothe the painful knot in his stomach. "Could we talk about something else?"

"Could we go back to sleep?" Thane yawned. "It's the middle of the night."

"I can't sleep. You get some rest." Corban got to his feet and headed to the ladder. "Goodnight." The other two offered no protest.

Corban descended in darkness, feeling for each rung with care, until he reached level four. The library's overhead sensor lights flickered on as he walked over to one of the study tables and dropped into a chair. His heart pounded from the nightmare. Corban hated feeling terrified, helpless, and confused. *The premonition has to be wrong. There has to be a logical explanation.* He couldn't imagine doing or saying anything to make Nikki angry enough to want to kill him.

He rested his chin on his hands and tried to relax, staring down at the tabletop, which was bare except for a few scraps of paper leftover from the last brainstorming session. He reached for one of the scraps and slid it close enough to read.

Allies

Names filled four columns in Zhao's small, precise handwriting. Under the *Lakeside* column were over one hundred names, including the mayor, which gave Corban some hope. The lists under *East Fort* and *West Fort* were short, and *Waterfall*'s list was the shortest, with Rupert Conquist and Robin Aziz's family written beneath it. At the bottom of the paper, question marks were jotted beneath *Greenfield* and *Orchard Valley*. It was frustrating to have no way to communicate with the other forts. It would take too much time to bike there and back, much less go door-to-door and talk to people.

Corban picked up the other scrap of paper. He already knew what was written on it, having compiled the list himself.

Enemies

It was long. *Mayor Mariposa Savoy, East Fort; Mayor Leighton Abrams, West Fort; Chaim Rajamani, Smiths Guild master; Kun Kaczenski, Herbalists Guild master; Elian Ramirez, Farmers Guild master.*

Corban paused as he considered Elian Ramirez. Nikki once mentioned she didn't have a hologram of her father because Solona destroyed them all. It was hard to comprehend a father heartless enough to abandon his own daughters, especially after so many colonists lost family members during the Plague.

He understood, just a little, why Leighton hated him and Thane. Uncle had told them many times how much he resented being stuck with two boys who weren't his sons. The fact that they were Strays only added fuel to Leighton's resentment. According to Uncle, he and Thane were unnatural, disgusting, and worthless. They had been despised and abused for sixteen storms for the crime of being different. *We didn't choose to be Strays. We can't change who we are.* He and Thane endured their miserable home life together, determined to escape when the circumstances were right.

Yet here we are in hiding, still trying to escape Leighton.

Then there was Nikki, who was like a ray of Ilios cutting through the darkness of his life.

Except he couldn't touch her. And she was going to kill him.

He didn't know what to think anymore. It was like living in an alternate reality, one where his future killer sat across the table from him with a dimpled smile, but all he could do was daydream about holding her in his arms, her lips pressed against his.

Then his imagination conjured up a vision of his headless body lying in the orchard grass, and he was forced to think about something else before he lost his mind.

***

A hand gripped Corban's shoulder, startling him. He sat straight up in the chair.

"Good morning. Sleep well?" Thane's tone was sympathetic, but laced with sarcasm.

"Ugh! Everything hurts!" Corban rubbed his aching jaw, which had been supporting his head on the tabletop. He noted with disgust the pattern of the wood grain embedded in his chin.

"Why didn't you move over to one of the couches?"

Corban shook off Thane's hand and struggled to stand. He staggered around the room for a minute, working off the pins and needles in his calves and feet. "Zhao still out?"

"I don't think you'll see him till midday." Thane sat and tied his boots. "I'll head over to West Fort while it's early."

"I wish I could do more to help." Corban massaged the knot at the small of his back. "I hate being stuck here by myself."

"Zhao's here," Thane said.

Corban shrugged. "Zhao's spends all day reading the datafiles."

"You're saying you can't compete with him intellectually?"

"Hey!"

Thane shot him a teasing grin. "Nikki and Jing should be here soon."

Corban's mood improved. "How do you know?"

"Derek just told me."

"Why doesn't Derek send me messages?"

"Nikki wanted it to be a surprise." Thane rolled his eyes and got to his feet.

"I don't need surprise visitors, not when I haven't showered in a week." Corban headed to the ladder, still stretching the kinks out of his aching back. "I'm going to wash up."

"I'll see you later." Thane shouldered his backpack and followed him. The brothers climbed in opposite directions.

The water from the ship's cistern was ice cold, but Corban lathered up at the bathroom sink, despite his chattering teeth. He swiped a razor over his chin, taking off the worst of the stubble, grateful the wood grain no longer left a pattern on his jaw.

He climbed to the top level, found his last clean pair of underwear in his duffle bag, and made a mental note to wash his clothes in the sink first chance he got. He selected his least-dirty pair of jeans and helped himself to Thane's last clean T-shirt.

Zhao rolled over in his blanket and glared up at him, annoyed at being disturbed, but Corban didn't apologize.

"Your sister will be here soon, and you smell like a trashbird."

"No one's gotten close enough to a trashbird to tell if they stink."

"They eat trash," Corban said. "Trust me, they stink, and so do you."

"Any water?"

Corban chuckled. "I left some in the sink."

"Gross. I don't want to bathe in water that had your butt in it."

"Then don't bathe in the toilet."

Zhao threw a rolled-up sock at him, but Corban was already on his way back down the ladder. He didn't have to wait long in the library before Nikki and Jing arrived.

"We brought food." Nikki flashed him a smile, but he was unable to return the greeting as a sense of foreboding hit hard. Corban's eyes were drawn to her clothes. She was wearing the same outfit from his premonition—a long-sleeve black T-shirt and faded blue jeans with rips in the knees. Her hair was even pulled back into a ponytail, and she never wore it up, at least not around him.

"Corban?" Nikki walked over to his table. "You have the same look on your face."

"What look?" He made an effort to shape his mouth into a smile, but he sensed her suspicion.

"The look you gave me the first time we met." She narrowed her eyes at him. "Like you'd seen a ghost."

"He was mesmerized by your beauty." Jing smirked, setting her bag on the table with a loud *thunk*.

The sound distracted Corban enough to tear his gaze from Nikki's face. "So what did you bring us?" He opened the bag, but Nikki loomed over him, moving closer so their eyes were centimeters apart.

"What's wrong?" she asked.

"I was mesmerized by your beauty, like Jing said."

Jing snorted and covered a laugh.

Nikki scowled at him, not budging.

Corban was tempted to lie, but he couldn't make himself do it. "You're wearing the same clothes I saw in the dream. And your hair is the same . . ." his voice trailed off.

Nikki stepped back. She was speechless for a moment, her lower lip quivering, but then she shook it off. He sensed her mood shift from nervousness to determination. "Who wants quiche? Eliana made us a gourmet breakfast." She turned away from him and took some items out of the bag.

"Thanks," Corban said. "I'm so hungry I could eat a night terror."

Neither of them mentioned the premonition for the rest of the day. Corban tried to focus on enjoying his time with Nikki, but a nagging thought in the back of his mind refused to go away. *Is this our last day together?*

***

Thane looked exhausted when he returned at dusk. He stepped off the ladder and limped over to the others. "Ms. Piroux left a bag of food for us at the exchange spot." He shrugged off his backpack and set it on the table.

"Good." Corban shoved the playing cards out of the way. "I'm starved."

"You're always starved, and you were losing." Jing raked her winnings—a small pile of pecans—into her hand and deposited them in her mouth.

"Was not." Corban held up his bag of pecans to show them he had three left.

Nikki opened the backpack and distributed a dinner of barbequed bluedeer sandwiches and apples to the others. "What did you hear?"

Zhao managed to drag himself away from his datafile station and join them at the table. "Any news?"

Thane pulled up a chair and sat down with a sigh. "You're not going to like it."

Everyone stopped what they were doing and gave him their full attention. Corban's sandwich was halfway to his mouth, his appetite already gone.

"The roundup takes place tomorrow."

"Darkness. That didn't take long. The mayors didn't even meet again to vote on the plan." Nikki's hand on her lap shifted to Corban's chair. She gripped the edge of the seat next to his hand, her intent clear, but her Talent, as usual, kept her from making contact.

Corban wrestled with the familiar sense of frustration but tried to keep his face a mask, for Nikki's sake, as he focused on Thane's words.

"They're moving forward with the plan, ahead of schedule, because of us. Uncle's worried that, given enough time, we might mount a successful counter offense. He's organized teams with trucks for each fort. They'll all be armed. Kun Kaczenski's leading one of the teams—"

Jing hissed like an angry purple crawler.

"—Chaim's leading another."

"Doesn't surprise me," Corban said.

"Plenty of others signed on to help."

"What can we do?" Jing scanned the other faces at the table. "Nikki?"

"We only got the word out to Lakeside, with Mayor Brooks and my mom's assistance. There's so few of us to make a difference—not when they've got weapons."

Thane nodded. "I heard a lot going on at the cache today. Several trucks stopped by the tree. Chaim helped distribute the guns."

"Ammo?" Zhao asked.

"That was distributed too, although I did hear Uncle say, 'Take a handful, only a handful. Don't use them unless you need to because I don't have any to spare.'"

"So it sounds like they won't be shooting up the place," Corban said, "but we should assume anyone with a gun is one of Uncle's soldiers."

"It only takes one bullet to kill someone." Jing set her half-eaten sandwich down, her face paler than usual.

"We need to take up observation posts inside one of the forts," Nikki said without conviction. "We might find a way to help."

"Rupert and Derek could send messages. I could go back to my post and listen to what's happening in West Fort," Thane said.

"No, you look beat. You need to take tomorrow morning off," Nikki said. "We'll go in shifts. Jing, Corban, and Rupert in the morning; me, you, and Zhao in the afternoon. Derek insists on watching the landing strip because Mom is paranoid something will happen to me. I don't know if he can help with messages."

"We need more binoculars," Corban said.

"Rupert and Derek have the only pairs we found," Thane said.

"What we need are Strays with seeing Talents paired with hearers like Thane, and more communicators like Rupert and Derek." Nikki nodded toward the datafile stations. "If we knew which Stray had which Talent, we could organize a resistance."

"I made a short list of Strays and their Talents," Zhao said. "I wrote down the names of people I know, so I was limited to Lakeside and my guild." He indicated the two scraps of paper on the other table.

"It's a start," Nikki told him. "Thanks for trying."

"But we're out of time to recruit more help from the other forts," Jing said.

"I know." Nikki picked up her sandwich, frowned at it, and put it back on the table without taking a bite.

Corban didn't need empathy to sense the worry and frustration from his teammates. He thought of them as a team, united in a common cause.

"Should Nik and I go back to Lakeside tonight?" Jing focused her gaze on Thane, as if appealing to him for a wise answer since he was the oldest, but Corban sensed an ulterior motive in her query.

She likes him?

Thane shook his head, not looking at her. "It's dark now."

"Mom knows where we are. She'll tell your dad you're staying at our apartment," Nikki said.

"*Baba* won't even miss me," Jing said. "He's been spending all his time recruiting soldiers for Leighton's army." She exchanged a worried frown with her brother. "I think he's been going to East Fort every day since all this mess started."

They ate in silence for a few minutes until Nikki spoke up. "We'd better get some sleep." She pushed aside her unfinished sandwich. "Which level do Jing and I want?"

"Eleven has a working bathroom," Corban said. "I've got an extra pillow and blanket. I'll bring them down to you." He studied Nikki's face for a reaction, but her expression was guarded. He sensed she was scared but determined to find the courage needed for what was to come.

The courage we all need.

"Bring down my extra pillow and blanket for Jing too." Thane averted his gaze as he spoke. Corban suspected his brother liked Jing, but for some reason he was doing his best to ignore her. He made a mental note to ask him about it when the crisis was over. *Assuming we all survive.*

Zhao seemed oblivious to the unspoken tension. "Goodnight, *mei mei*." He gave his sister a peck on the cheek and headed to the ladder.

Corban followed Zhao and ascended to the top level.

"I've got a clean towel." Zhao dug through his pile of paraphernalia and handed Corban a bar of soap too.

"Thanks." He bundled everything under one arm and climbed down to level eleven.

Jing and Nikki were waiting for him at the ladder. Jing took the bedding and towel from him and said goodnight.

Nikki waited until Jing walked back toward the bathroom before whispering, "I'd kiss you goodnight, if I could."

Corban made an effort to keep the frustration out of his tone. "I know."

"Tomorrow"—she took a deep breath— "tomorrow is going to be horrible. Your uncle, Jing's father, my father—"

"I promise I won't let anything happen to you."

"It's not me I'm worried about." Nikki's lower lip trembled. "No matter what happens, it doesn't change the fact that one day I'm going to come after you in the peach orchard and—" She stifled a sob and turned away.

Corban wanted to take her in his arms, but all he could do was rub his thumb against a patch of rust on the ladder. "We have to believe the premonition was wrong. It won't happen."

"You said they're never wrong." Nikki was too choked up to continue. "Goodnight, Corban." She made her way toward the dark recesses of the eleventh level.

He watched her go, convinced he had never felt such despair. Not even a brutal beating by Leighton left him feeling this low. Corban gripped the rungs and climbed up to the nose cone.

Thane arrived a few minutes later. "I put the leftovers in the fridge," was his excuse for dallying. He sat on his bedroll and took his time removing his brace.

Zhao was already curled up in his blanket with his eyes closed, but Corban suspected he was feigning sleep. How could any of them sleep, knowing what was going to happen tomorrow?

"Goodnight." Thane lay back on his pillow and stared up at the ceiling.

Corban found the light switch and crawled across the cold deck plates to find his bedroll in the dark. "Goodnight."

***

He was standing on the far side of the wide bridge, looking toward the landing strip, when it happened.

The explosion knocked him backward, off his feet. Corban watched in horror as a geyser of fire shot skyward. In moments, the landing strip was engulfed in clouds of smoke. He couldn't see any of the ships, or the bridge or the river, the smoke was so thick.

Coughing, he sat up, eyes watering as he squinted though the haze, trying to make out which ship was on fire, but it was impossible to tell. Fire raged over the entire tarmac, flames licking the sky. Whichever ship exploded, it had obliterated most of the others.

***

Corban sat up, gasping in horror.

"What? What is it?" It was Zhao's voice.

Thane scrambled to Corban's side and put a firm hand on his shoulder. His eyes were wide with concern as he peered into Corban's face. "What? What did you see?"

"I think I saw the end of the colony."

SEVENTEEN
ROUNDUP

Corban wasn't himself. He looked shaken and refused to tell Nikki what was wrong. She suspected the roundup wasn't what troubled him. She couldn't fathom what it would be like to see the future and live in constant fear with that knowledge. She wished he hadn't told her about the sword premonition or pointed out yesterday that she was wearing the same clothes from his dream. She didn't have any other clothes to change into to reduce his stress level.

"Jing and I should get going if we want to get to the rooftop without being seen." Corban didn't make eye contact with Nikki.

"Rupert told me he was already on his way to West Fort." Thane was as grim-faced as his brother. "He'll take the east wall, and he suggested you take the west."

"Right over Uncle's apartment," Corban said. "What could be easier? I should be able to get inside the fort if the sentries are involved with the roundup, but in case they're still looking for me—" He pulled on the baggy jacket Thane used for his old man disguise. He found the dark glasses and folding cane in the pockets, slipped on the glasses, and unfolded the walking stick. "How do I look? Should I whiten my hair too?"

"I think you'll pass." Jing used both hands to muss Corban's hair until it stuck up all over, as if he had been out in a storm.

Thane ran a hand over his new crew cut and clean-shaven jaw. "I wish I had that option when we went to Waterfall."

"Sorry." Jing sounded sincere, but Nikki suspected she preferred Thane's new look. The bruises beneath his eyes were almost gone, and the crooked nose made him appear more rugged, like a wrestler or bodyguard.

Corban didn't touch any of the pastries or fruit Nikki set out on the table for their breakfast. He said, "Come on, Jing," and headed toward the ladder.

Mayor Brooks has Lakeside on lockdown. Nikki sat up straight in her chair. "What?"

"I said, 'Come on, Jing.'" Corban looked confused.

"No, not you. Derek told me Mayor Brooks has Lakeside on lockdown."

"What does it mean?" Jing asked.

I can leave but can't get back in. She has all her sentries at the gates. The doors are barricaded and no one gets in without her authorization. Nikki repeated Derek's message to the others.

"She's fighting back!" Jing said. "She won't let the Strays be taken today!"

Nikki whooped. "I always knew I liked that woman."

"But Uncle has guns," Corban said.

172

"Guns can't break through locked gates." Thane smiled for the first time in days. "I wonder if she'll let us take refuge there."

"If we survive the day," Zhao said, "every Stray in the colony will take refuge in Lakeside."

Thanks for crushing our hopes. Nikki exchanged a frown with Jing. "We *will* survive the day!"

Jing nodded, but she looked scared. She gave Zhao a kiss on the cheek. "Goodbye, *ge'-ge',*" and added a hasty, "I love you," before following Corban to the ladder. "See you all at midday." She didn't sound optimistic.

"Please be careful," Nikki called after them, wishing she could hug her best friend and her boyfriend goodbye. *In case they don't come back.* She sat at the table with Thane and Zhao. They exchanged worried frowns, but Nikki didn't know what to say.

***

"Someone's at the airlock!" Thane leapt to his feet. "Get upstairs, quick!"

The blood drained from Nikki's face as she dashed to the ladder behind Zhao. "They'll hear us, they'll hear us," she whimpered to herself as she ascended.

Zhao got off on level six. "Go up to the next level," he said before she stepped off to join him. "Hide. Maybe they won't catch all of us." She detected no optimism in his tone.

Thane was right on Nikki's heels, hopping rung to rung on his right foot. Nikki kept climbing, her eyes riveted on Zhao's tense face until she reached level seven. She didn't wait to see where Thane got off but rushed forward to find a place to hide.

Level seven contained a single kitchenette and six bulkhead storage lockers. Nikki yanked open a lower locker. It was empty and small, but she didn't have time to be choosy. She squeezed herself inside and pulled the door shut, hoping for enough air to sustain her for a few minutes.

Why did I tell Zhao to hide my sword? A weapon was the only thing her terror-filled mind could focus on in the darkness. She wanted a way to defend herself. The sword was no match against rifles, but she wasn't ready to be hauled away to Seventh Fort, not yet. Whether Leighton Abrams considered his creation an internment camp or a prison didn't matter in her mind. She knew he intended to separate the Strays from the rest of the colony and was prepared to use force to do it.

Abrams is headed to the library to get a copy of the Stray directory from the datafiles. Rupert's warning came five minutes too late, but it offered Nikki a morsel of hope.

Maybe he didn't hear us on the ladder. Maybe he'll get a copy of the list and leave.

Her *maybe* turned out to be wishful thinking when she heard a commotion on the level below. Muffled shouts and the unmistakable *crack* of a gunshot made her blood run cold. *Zhao!*

She pressed her elbow against the cabinet door, but it wouldn't budge. She ran her fingers over the panel, searching for a latch or handle, but found nothing but a smooth, blank surface. It was designed to be opened from the outside. *Darkness!* Nikki threw her shoulder against the door. She heard it creak in protest, but it remained shut.

The shouts were coming closer. She heard Leighton Abrams's voice, but there were others she didn't recognize. Since she was outnumbered, unarmed, and trapped in the locker, common sense dictated she remain silent to avoid being discovered.

Another gunshot, it sounded closer. She began to hyperventilate, knowing it was the worst thing to do in an enclosed space. *Breathe, breathe, calm down.*

"Uncle!" Thane sounded terrified. She heard someone cry out in pain.

"Get them down to the airlock!" Abrams shouted.

More commotion on the ladder and another cry of pain. Nikki couldn't tell who was hurt. Her nerves were stretched as taut as guitar strings. She wanted to scream, but she battled to keep her nerves under control, biting down on her lip until she tasted blood.

Not knowing what was happening outside the cabinet was the worst thing Nikki ever experienced, worse than being tied up and locked in the cellar. *Zhao? Thane?* Were they hurt? Did Abrams shoot them? Tears leaked from the corners of her eyes as she listened and waited.

And waited.

The shouts and commotion were moving away from her position, growing fainter until she strained her ears to hear anything. Then all she heard was silence.

Nikki, stay where you are, Derek's familiar voice spoke to her mind. *Abrams has Zhao and Thane, but he's leaving the ship without you. I heard shots, but I assume you're still alive*—she thought she detected a catch in his voice—*stay put and we'll come for you as soon as it's safe.*

He's rounding up the Strays. Rupert's voice came to her fifteen minutes later. *Abrams is at West Fort. They're going door-to-door. He has a list . . .*

Nikki was light-headed. She wasn't sure if it was from the shock or the lack of oxygen. She shifted as best she could in the tiny space until she was able to wedge her knees against the back wall. Using her legs as leverage, she pressed her shoulders against the door.

The door popped open and Nikki fell backward onto the cold deck plates. She sucked in a lungful of fresh air before climbing to her feet. She was drenched with sweat, shaking and nauseated, but she paused to listen before moving to the ladder.

She listened again before reaching out to grasp the rungs. The ship was silent. She stepped off at level six, scanning the floor with her eyes. She didn't want to admit to herself she was looking for traces of blood, but she needed to know.

Her stomach unclenched a fraction when she didn't find any blood. A bullet hole pierced the door to the bathroom, but it was the sole evidence a struggle had taken place.

Nikki hesitated again at the ladder. Derek advised her to stay put, but she knew she would lose her mind if she didn't do something to help Zhao and Thane.

I gave Zhao the sword. I told him to hide it. The answer was so obvious, she almost laughed at her own stupidity. *Zhao lives on the ship with Corban and Thane.*

Nikki ascended the ladder to the top level. The small, cone-shaped room contained three bedrolls, arranged on the floor in a rough triangle, and three piles of belongings, mostly clothes. She recognized Corban's tattered copy of *Bushcraft: Outdoor Survival Guide* on top of one pile and skipped over it. Thane's water bottle perched next to another bundle, so she ignored it too. She knelt by Zhao's pile and searched but turned up nothing.

Impatience drove caution from her mind. She grabbed the bedroll next to Zhao's clothes and threw it aside.

Relief flooded her. She wouldn't have to search the entire ship.

Nikki picked up the long sword by the hilt and stuck the blade through the belt loop on the left side of her jeans where the cross guard held it in place. The fabric threatened to separate from the weight of the weapon, but she didn't take time to improvise something better. There was no time to lose.

EIGHTEEN
PRISONER

Thane was sure he had a cracked a rib, but he was more concerned about Zhao. Jing's brother had a concussion. He vomited the moment Uncle and his soldiers hauled them outside the airlock, and he threw up again when the group reached the tarmac at the bottom of the gangway.

"Take him to Seventh!" Leighton ordered the driver of the truck waiting next to the ship. The men half-carrying Zhao deposited him in the truck bed where he joined eight terrified-looking passengers Thane didn't recognize.

One of the captive Strays reached over to help Zhao, but a familiar voice snapped, "Get away from him and sit down!"

Thane recognized the guard from the dining hall the night he rushed to rescue Corban and Nikki. The sentry was sitting next to the driver, holding a rifle on the group, the muzzle poking out of the cab through the back window.

"Sit down!" she said. "Let's move!"

"Zhao!" Thane wanted to break free of his escorts, but the stabbing pain in his chest kept him immobilized. "Let me go with him!" he shouted at Leighton.

A backhanded blow snapped Thane's head to one side, silencing him faster than any verbal threat his uncle could make.

"No, you're coming with me." Uncle gripped the back of Thane's neck with one hand and forced his head to turn until their eyes were level. "You're my leverage to make sure the Strays do as they're told."

Leighton's smirk turned menacing. "I'm on a tight schedule today, so why don't you tell me where your worthless brother is?"

Thane did something he had always wanted to do. He spat in his uncle's face.

The punch in the mouth he received was worth it. Thane tasted blood but didn't care. He wasn't afraid of Leighton, not anymore. "You'll never find him. Corban foresaw this weeks ago. That's why you're scared of him. His Talent for seeing the future was always a threat to your plans. You're delusional if you think you can lock up the Strays now that the whole colony knows."

Leighton laughed. "I'm not the one who's delusional! You think I'm afraid of Corban? I've got news for you. We're locking you up, all of you—today!"

A second truck pulled up to the gangway, driven by Kun Kaczenski. Thane felt a pang of sympathy for Jing. They shared something unfortunate in common—family members willing to betray them for being different. In Jing's case, she was simply defending her brother and her best friend. She didn't

179

deserve to be treated like a criminal—none of them did.

There were no Strays in Kun's truck. *Not yet,* Thane thought.

"Did you get the list?" Kaczenski asked Uncle.

Leighton drew a sheaf of papers from the cargo pocket of his jeans. "I have addresses. Let's make sure they purge all the Strays from West Fort."

Thane's silent handlers dragged him over to the tailgate and shoved him into the truck bed. He was in too much pain to put up a fight, but they ensured his cooperation by tying his hands in front of him with a piece of rope. Then the two men sat in the bed on either side of him, rifles propped beside them.

"If he tries to escape, shoot him." Leighton climbed into the cab, next to Kun. "Let's go."

NINETEEN
HOSTAGE

From the roof of the west wall, Corban peered between a pair of battlements and watched in silent fury as young people were marched to trucks at gunpoint. Despite Uncle's confidence the Strays would go willingly, fist fights erupted all over the grounds of West Fort. Strays used their Talents to resist armed men and women foolish enough to do Leighton's bidding. Normals and some Survivors were fighting to defend their friends and family members. It was chaos.

Corban wanted to do something to help, but people were getting hurt. Which skirmish to join? He knew it was a matter of time before someone got nervous, pulled a trigger, and a real war broke out.

A truck loaded with Strays drove away from a crowd of protesters and exited the gates. Moments later, an empty truck drove in to replace it.

No, the truck wasn't empty. Thane was in the back between two armed men.

Thane! Rupert's voice shouted in Corban's mind. *He looks hurt!*

181

Corban wished he had a way to respond. He squinted across the fort to the east wall but couldn't make out anything. Rupert had the team's sole pair of binoculars, and he was too far away to help.

The truck stopped on the street beneath Corban, and Leighton climbed out of the passenger's seat. The driver hopped out to join him, a rifle slung over his shoulder.

Corban wondered if Jing, who was doing her stakeout on the north wall, was close enough to see her father taking part in the roundup.

They're going inside the west wall.

I can see, Rhubarb, I'm not blind. Corban was grateful he held off joining the hand-to-hand combat because now he had an opportunity to rescue Thane before his uncle returned to the truck.

Threading the maze of rain barrels and solar panels, Corban hurried back to the roof access door, which descended to the third floor hallway. The chaos in the apartment hallways was worse than the commotion in the streets. He took the stairs two at a time, dodging people of all ages who were fleeing the building ahead of Uncle's armed zealots.

"No! You can't take her!" Emily Vaughn's shrill voice rose above the shouts and confusion.

Corban stopped short on the second floor landing and felt as if his heart split in half. He hesitated a moment, weighing two impossible choices before making a decision he knew he might regret. *Sorry, Thane.* He sprinted down the hallway, pushing people out of the way to reach apartment 21W.

His teacher attempted to barricade the open doorway to her apartment with her tiny body. "She's a special case! She's not well! She can't leave the apartment! You can't take her! I won't let you!"

A high-pitched shriek came from behind Ms. Vaughn. "Darkness! Make the darkness go away, Mama!"

"You can't take her! It'll kill her!" Ms. Vaughn's eyes found Corban's in the crowd. "Tell him! Tell him Brida can't leave!"

Corban pushed closer, trying to get to his uncle, who was attempting to get past Emily Vaughn. "Leave her alone! Uncle, she's disturbed! She can't go outside!"

If he hoped his sudden appearance would distract Leighton, he was mistaken. The mayor was obsessed with reaching the hysterical Stray, the child-like woman with Down syndrome.

"Get out of the way." Leighton shoved Ms. Vaughn aside, forcing his way into the apartment.

Corban pushed his way past Kun Kaczenski and rushed to aid Ms. Vaughn. She had a death grip on Uncle's right arm, preventing him from pointing his pistol at Brida.

"Get off me!" Leighton slapped Ms. Vaughn with his free hand, knocking her to the floor before Corban hit him in a flying tackle.

They collided with the couch and rolled off onto the floor, with Leighton on the bottom. Corban managed to get both hands around his uncle's wrist. Once again, they fought for possession of a weapon.

Brida's screams increased in volume. She was running around the sitting room, tearing at her hair, sobbing and hysterical. "Mama! Make the darkness go away!"

Ms. Vaughn struggled to her feet and attacked the two soldiers who came in behind Corban to assist

Leighton. She snatched up a table lamp and swung it, hitting them anywhere she could reach.

Corban was dimly aware of what else was going on in the room as he strained every muscle in his arms. Despite his efforts, the barrel of Uncle's pistol came closer and closer to his forehead.

"You should've died that night outside the fort," Leighton hissed. "Worthless Stray."

Summoning all his strength, Corban forced the barrel away from his face a heartbeat before Uncle pulled the trigger.

The noise was so loud, Corban thought both eardrums imploded. Ms. Vaughn was screaming, but the sound was muffled. *Was she hit?* He pushed away from Leighton and staggered to his feet, looking around wildly to see if someone had been shot.

Someone had. Corban fell to his knees next to the still form of Brida Vaughn.

"Murderer!" Ms. Vaughn's scream pierced the sudden silence. "You killed my daughter!"

Corban stared at the bright red puddle expanding beneath Brida. The ringing in his ears muffled the other sounds in the room. He wanted to reach out to Ms. Vaughn and comfort her, but in the shock and confusion, he forgot there was one big problem to deal with.

Leighton seized him by the hair and dragged him to his feet. In one swift movement, he twisted Corban's left arm behind his back and jammed the barrel of the pistol between his shoulder blades. He forced Corban to walk ahead of him to the doorway.

I left Thane! I didn't help anyone, and now I'm a hostage! Corban sensed the anxiety in each person he passed, from a sobbing Ms. Vaughn, from the soldiers who came to assist Leighton and were now unnerved by the violence they had witnessed, from the silent crowd of his neighbors and classmates in the hallway.

His uncle marched him down the hall, down the stairwell, and toward the truck. Kun Kaczenski fell into step next to Corban, rifle at the ready, escorting Leighton from the building.

The truck bed was empty. Thane was nowhere in sight.

Corban felt a flutter of hope. *Thane escaped? Did Rupert and Jing rescue him?*

Can they rescue me in time? Leighton forced him into the cab, next to Kaczenski in the driver's seat. Corban focused on his uncle's emotions, but sensed nothing. The anger he normally wielded had been replaced with something more terrifying—a void.

He tried to kill me and almost succeeded. What did he say before he shot Brida? I should've died outside the fort that night? An icy hand reached inside Corban's chest and wrapped an iron fist around his heart. Details from his fractured memory began to make sense in his mind. *He set us up! He sent me outside the fort, then sent Thane to find me. He tried to kill both of us.*

In that moment, Corban knew Leighton didn't intend to take him to Seventh Fort with the other captive Strays. The mayor had another plan for his nephew. *A permanent plan.*

Leighton squeezed in next to him, the pistol wedged against Corban's side. The truck started and Kaczenski drove through the gates.

The two men argued with each other, but the loud buzzing in Corban's ears prevented him from hearing their words. He watched the road and tried to push the image of Brida's lifeless body from his mind. He thought of Nikki and Thane, and wished he could say goodbye to them.

Rupert's voice broke through the gloom of Corban's thoughts. *Thane heard them say they're taking you to the peach orchard. That's where Nikki's dad stockpiled more ammo.*

Corban was so cold he couldn't breathe. *I'm going to die. And Nikki's going to be the one to kill me.*

TWENTY
RESCUE

Thane counted thirty seconds from the moment his uncle and Jing's father disappeared inside the stairwell of the west wall to the moment Ms. Piroux and her daughter Dagmar appeared at the tailgate of the truck. Ms. Piroux's wild gray spirals matched her daughter's ink-black ringlets, and both women wore intimidating scowls on their dark brown faces.

"Don't you gentlemen have something better to do?" Ms. Piroux got the soldiers' attention by shaking her cleaver at them.

Thane's guards gaped at her in alarm, but when they glanced down at their laps, they both gasped. They scrambled to their feet, searching the truck bed.

"Where's my gun?" one asked.

The other one said, in a panicky voice, "It was right here beside me!"

"Some guards you are." Dagmar smirked.

"Since you're unarmed, you might want to leave before that crowd rips you apart." Ms. Piroux pointed with her cleaver at the flood of colonists exiting the door to the west wall staircase.

"They look really angry to me." Dagmar could barely contain a laugh.

The soldiers exchanged a look of dismay before climbing over the sides of the truck and hurrying away.

The crowd from the west wall scattered, ignoring Thane and the two women.

"That took too long." Dagmar hopped into the back where the two rifles were now visible on the floor. She handed one to her mother before untying Thane's hands.

"Thank you." Thane took Dagmar's proffered hand, and she pulled him to his feet. He winced at the stabbing pain in his right side.

"Thank your friend Rupert for sending me a message." Ms. Piroux ejected the magazine from the rifle and snorted in disgust. "No bullets! This isn't a coup, it's a flock of trashbirds trying to act tough!"

Dagmar picked up the other rifle, ejected the magazine to confirm it was also empty, and she and Thane climbed down from the truck bed.

"Thane!" Jing came barreling down the cobbled street toward him, arms wide open.

Oh, no. Thane turned his body so she embraced his left side. He let out a gasp of pain and almost fell.

"I'm sorry!" Jing tried to steady him, but he extended his free arm to get her to step back. "Did I hurt you?"

"No, Uncle did. I've got a busted rib."

"Where's Zhao? Where's Nikki?"

"I think they took him to Seventh." Thane steadied himself by gripping the truck's side. He tried taking shallow breaths, gritting his teeth against the pain. "They didn't find Nikki. I think she's still in the library."

A gunshot sounded from inside the west wall, and a sudden, eerie silence fell over the entire fort.

Jing's hand found Thane's. She was shaking. "Did someone—?"

Thane was almost afraid to listen, but he tuned his ears. What he heard shook him to the core. He peered into Ms. Piroux's worried face. "Brida's dead."

"No!" The cook choked back a cry. "And Emily?"

"She's safe." Thane blocked out Ms. Vaughn's screams to keep his own emotions in check. "My uncle shot Brida."

With a start, he realized they didn't have time to mourn. "Uncle's coming outside! He's got Corban! We need to hide!"

The little group was in motion, heading across the street toward the dining hall. Jing pulled Thane's left arm across her shoulders and helped him walk, taking care not to jostle his right side. People gave the Pirouxes a wide berth when they noticed both women carried rifles. They were able to get inside the abandoned dining hall before Leighton, Jing's father, and Corban emerged from the west wall stairwell.

Thane pressed his face to the front window of the dining room, watching in fear as Uncle forced his brother at gunpoint into the truck cab between Kaczenski and himself.

"What'll we do?" Jing gripped Thane's hand tighter. "Where're they taking him?"

Thane shut his eyes, listening. "Darkness! They're taking him to the peach orchard!" He turned to Jing. "You've got to find Rupert! He's the only one who can send word."

"To Nikki?" The worry and confusion on Jing's features reflected his own.

The knot in Thane's stomach hurt more than the pain from his rib. "I don't know. Just tell Rupert to warn them."

"I'll go with you," Dagmar offered.

"I'll take care of Thane." Ms. Piroux nodded, tears streaming down her face.

"Thank you." Jing sent Thane an expression he was unable to decipher before hurrying out of the dining hall with Dagmar Piroux

***

Thane was numb inside as Ms. Piroux tried to make him comfortable. He sat on a table while the Cooks Guild master wrapped a roll of heavy gauze around his bare chest.

"Sorry, it'll have to be tight to immobilize the rib." She studied his face with concern before reaching into her first aid kit, searching its meager contents. "I think I have one more analgesic patch. It's not much, but it'll take the edge off the pain."

Thane nodded, grateful for some relief, and she applied the patch to his neck, behind his right ear.

"I can't believe she's gone." Ms. Piroux's eyes leaked tears. "She had such a sweet disposition, like an angel."

"I'm sorry my uncle's a son of a—"

"It's all right," she interrupted. "No need for that kind of language."

"Yes, ma'am. Thank you for rescuing me, again. Tell Dagmar thank you."

She nodded absentmindedly as she peered out the window. "It seems to have calmed down since the shooting. I should go find Emily."

Thane agreed. He stood with care and watched her leave through the dining hall's double doors. His mind raced as he found his shirt and managed to get it over his head one-handed. He hated being stuck here, unable to do anything to help Corban. *What's going to happen when they reach the peach orchard?*

It all came down to Corban's premonition. The thought of the young woman Thane had come to know and respect getting a sudden urge to decapitate his brother didn't make sense. It was obvious Corban and Nikki had feelings for each other, although it was hard to define their relationship since they couldn't touch.

Thane limped to the door and peered out at the street. Ms. Piroux was right; the fort was quieter since the shooting. He stepped outside and looked around.

Groups of young men and women were being loaded into trucks at gunpoint, but they weren't fighting back. People watched them leave with somber faces. It was too quiet. Thane headed toward the east wall, hoping to spot Rupert and Jing.

"Thane!" Jing raced toward him before he reached the end of the street. She was flushed and sweaty, but he thought it looked good on her. She stopped in front of him and forced a grin before reaching out to take his hand. "I found Rupert and he sent a message to Corban and Nikki."

"Where is he?" Thane looked around.

"He's still on the wall, sending the message to anyone he knows."

"What message?" He looked up, searching for his friend between the battlements.

"'All Strays should evacuate to Seventh Fort to prevent further loss of life.'"

Thane's jaw dropped. "We're giving up?"

Jing bit her lip. "We can't win, not this way. The cost is too high."

A fresh wave of bitterness washed over Thane. "My uncle should be the one banished. He murdered an innocent woman."

"I know," Jing whispered. "But it's better to survive to fight another day. The Strays have to get organized like Nikki said."

"Where's Nikki? Is she going to the—?" He was unable to utter the word 'orchard.'

"Derek told me she left the library and took my bike." Jing looked away. "She's headed south—and she's got the sword."

"I need to find Corban." Thane squeezed her hand, grateful for her presence.

"We'll need a ride." Jing looked determined. "You're not going into exile without me."

Thane frowned but didn't argue the point. They looked around and spotted a truck parked in front of the school. They started toward it when Rupert told him, *Wait for me. I'm coming too.*

***

"Are you Strays?" The armed woman standing next to the truck appraised Thane, Jing, and Rupert with a contemptuous scowl.

"Yes, we are," Jing said. "And my boyfriend's hurt, so he needs to ride in the cab."

Rupert shot Thane an incredulous look over the top of Jing's head. Thane sent a warning scowl in return.

"Everyone rides in the back," the woman said, stony-faced.

192

"I'll manage," Thane whispered to Jing, who looked angry enough to draw blood.

Rupert and Jing climbed onto the tailgate, and each took an arm to help Thane up. Wincing, he sat between them, resigning himself to a painful ride.

Jing pressed against his left side. "Lean on me. I'll try to brace you when we go over bumps."

"You don't have to do this. You're Normal. You don't have to go to Seventh Fort with me—with us."

"Yes, I do."

"You deserve better," Thane whispered. "You deserve someone who's not crippled."

Jing glared up at him with an expression so ferocious he knew he had crossed a line, but before he was able to apologize, she said, "We'll discuss it later, Thane Abrams, after we find my brother."

"Yes, ma'am." Thane frowned at Rupert, who rolled his eyes, having heard every word of their exchange. "Don't. Say. A word," he mouthed to his friend.

Who, me? Rupert replied. *I won't say something in front of you girlfriend. She might snap my neck like a twig.*

Thane was too exhausted and worried about Corban to laugh. He suspected any attempt to laugh would be painful anyway.

TWENTY-ONE
RACE

We told you to wait. Derek's tone echoed frustration, but Nikki didn't give him a second thought. She was too busy running.

Don't let me down, Jing. Nikki reached the far side of the bridge and slid down the weed-filled embankment. A pile of branches next to the river concealed Jing's bike from view. *She remembered!*

Nikki hauled the bike up to the road and hopped on, pedaling hard, the sword bouncing against her leg. She was grateful the road to Seventh Fort was mostly downhill because she wanted strength left to fight when she met Leighton Abrams.

The colony was in chaos. A few trucks, beds filled with captive Strays, went by her on the road, but it seemed no one was going to Seventh without a struggle. She was alarmed to see a truck in the ditch near Waterfall, but when she slowed to see if anyone was hurt, she received another surprise.

Four young women in purple Cooks Guild aprons were sitting on the driver and a uniformed sentry. Their captors were face-down on the side of the road, arms tied behind their backs, and the cooks were using them as couches. One of the women waved to Nikki and called, "Sorry we don't have a gun to loan you, but Siripimone threw it in the river."

"Thanks, but I'm covered." Nikki patted her sword and kept pedaling.

Twenty minutes later she reached the fork in the road which led to Seventh Fort, and Derek's warning reached her. *Abrams has Corban now, and he's taking him to the peach orchard. I don't know what Abrams is planning to do to Corban, but he just murdered Brida Vaughn.*

Nikki gasped. In her shock, she took her eyes off the road and ran into a log. The bike flipped over, and it was by luck or divine intervention that she didn't fall on the sword when she landed on her back in the ditch. With the wind knocked out of her, it took her a few minutes to get up. She eyed her skinned knees and bleeding elbow, and blotted the blood from the bigger cuts with her T-shirt.

She examined the sword first. It was fine. It tore through the belt loop and landed a meter away from her in the brush. Next, she looked at the bike, but the frame was bent. The front tire was mashed into an oblong shape. She needed to go the rest of the way on foot.

Her leg muscles quivered in protest as she jogged, but she intended to run as soon as her body agreed to shake off the bike wreck. She held the sword in her right hand since she didn't have a way to secure it to her clothes.

A harrowing image filled her mind as she recalled Corban's description of his premonition. *I'm not running into the orchard to kill Corban. I'm not.* Her mind screamed at her to stop, but she remembered

Abrams's hands around Corban's neck and knew she didn't have a choice. She had to save him.

He killed Brida! Tears came, unbidden, as she ran, blurring her vision as she hopped the split-rail fence and cut across the goat pasture. She stumbled a few times, blinded by grief, but kept running, determined to gain the first grove of fruit trees before Leighton's truck reached the road at the top of the hill behind her. If he saw her, she wouldn't be able to save Corban. The element of surprise was her only advantage.

Saving him, not killing him. But he saw me swing the sword! He felt the blade against his neck! Her leg muscles cramped. She wanted to collapse and give up. She wanted to die. Better to drop dead than for her to kill Corban. *But his uncle will kill him if I don't.* She was too distressed to wrestle with her own flawed logic.

The sputter of an electric engine reached her ears a moment after she vaulted the fence and tore into the apple grove. The beauty of the trees brought her a glimmer of hope. The gnarled, twisted branches were covered in cheerful white blossoms from the first growing season after the storm. *The driver didn't see me. There's still a chance.*

The road to Orchard Valley skirted the edges of the fruit groves. Half a kilometer before the gates of the fort was a stone barn off to the side of the road. It was used to shelter goats and sheep during the night. It also stood at the edge of the peach orchard, and it was probably where Abrams would park his truck. Nikki heard the truck coming down the hill, separated from her by half a dozen trees on her right.

A searing stitch in her side forced her to slow down, but she pushed through the pain. She heard the truck pull ahead. It would reach the peach orchard ahead of her. *I'm too late!*

TWENTY-TWO
MISSING PIECE

Corban watched the white-blossomed apple orchard merge into nut groves, grape arbors, cherry, pears, plums, and citrus trees, fig and olive bushes, and last of all, peach trees. He saw the stone barn ahead and felt as if his brain and body had parted ways. *Nikki won't show up here. It's impossible.* Rupert hadn't told him where she was, and Derek sent a vague message fifteen minutes earlier, *Hang on, we'll get a truck and try to reach you soon.*

Who is 'we'? How soon is 'soon'?

The buzzing sound filled his ears, drowning out Leighton's words to Kun as the guild master pulled up next to the barn and cut the engine. Uncle grabbed Corban's arm and dragged him from the cab. He indicated with the pistol the way Corban should go and walked behind him into the blossom-covered trees.

Corban focused on putting one foot in front of the other. His mind was blank. The sensation of déjà vu hit him, as it always did whenever one of his premonitions became a reality, but this time he didn't care. He knew the sword premonition was his last.

What about the dream from last night? How could you witness that if you're going to die in a few minutes? He wanted to hang onto a thread of hope, but it didn't seem possible.

Leighton spotted Nikki first, running toward them through the grove. He seized the back of Corban's shirt and shoved the pistol against his neck. "Hold it! Stop right there!"

The words were muffled, but Corban saw they had no effect on Nikki. She kept coming, her expression of rage exactly as he remembered. He even felt the blade against his neck.

No, I feel Uncle's gun against my neck! The missing piece of the puzzle fell into place.

"Stop or I'll shoot!" Leighton screamed.

Nikki was ten meters in front of them and closing fast.

He sensed Leighton's panic. His uncle let go of him, took a step back, and pointed the gun at her. "Stop!"

She raised the sword in both hands, closed the space between them with one last stride, and swung the blade straight at Corban, who was ready.

He ducked and the long blade passed over him. It struck Leighton, taking his head off his shoulders.

Nikki collided with Corban, unable to stop. Since he was bent down, she slammed into the top of his head, knocking him backward. Her momentum pitched her to the side, and she landed on her back in the grass next to Leighton's head.

Corban's neck ached from the impact, but he scrambled to his feet to get off Leighton's body. Nikki sat up, sobbing and almost hysterical. He offered her a hand and was astonished she accepted, but she had another surprise in store for him.

He helped her to her feet, and she threw her arms around him. She was gasping for breath, exhausted, filthy, and shaking all over, but she pressed her mouth to his without hesitation.

Corban couldn't help but respond. This was impossible, something he only imagined. He had no intention of spoiling the moment by figuring out how or why.

But he sensed something else, something strange. He heard a voice in his mind, but it wasn't Rupert's or Derek's—it was *Nikki's* voice. He broke off the kiss and took a hasty step back from her. Her voice inside his head vanished the moment they broke contact. "What happened?"

She blinked at him as if waking up from a deep sleep. He remembered her doing this after Jing and Solona hugged her.

"Did you know?" It was the most pressing question in Corban's mind. "Did you know I was going to duck?"

She nodded but her response was muted.

"What? I can't hear you."

Nikki raised her voice. "I saw it in your eyes, right before I swung. Is something wrong with your hearing?"

"Uncle shot Brida, and the gun was right next to my ear."

Her shoulders slumped. "So it's true? He murdered Brida?"

"It was an accident. He was aiming for me."

Nikki clamped a hand over her mouth as if she needed to vomit. Corban didn't think she could handle one more shock, so he switched her focus to something positive. "You can touch me now? What's changed?"

"I took Brida's advice." She shook her head. "Let's discuss it later. We need to rescue Thane—"

"Rupert or Jing already did."

"What about Zhao?"

"I don't know."

"I saw truckloads of Strays being taken to Seventh Fort. He's probably there. We have to get him out."

Corban turned to stare at Leighton's body and they were silent for a moment, taking in the grisly sight. He expected to see more blood.

"I should feel guilty for killing him, but all I feel is relief."

"Me too. The nightmare is finally over, and I didn't die." He looked into her eyes with a heartfelt, "Thank you."

Nikki forced a grin. "Thank you for ducking in time. Why didn't the slime worm shoot me?"

Corban stepped around the headless corpse and picked up the pistol near the right hand. He ejected the magazine. "This is why. It's empty."

"Rupert said he was bringing you here because there's a cache of ammunition."

A wave of bitterness swept over Corban. "His gun wasn't loaded! I could've escaped anytime if I'd known he used his last bullet on Brida!" He shoved the empty magazine back into the handgun and tucked the weapon into his cargo pocket. "I guess he was planning to reload it and shoot me here."

"Where's the ammo?" Nikki scanned the grove with her eyes.

"It could be anywhere if it's buried, but we don't have time to search."

"Is Jing's father still in the truck?" Nikki picked up the sword from the grass. She grimaced at the dark red blood on the blade but wiped it off using the hem of her T-shirt. "I'm already a mess," she responded to Corban's unasked question.

"Nikki, something strange happened when we kissed."

She gave him an incredulous look. "Was it that bad? I've never kissed anyone before."

A laugh almost escaped him, but he managed to turn it into a cough and keep a straight face. "No! I don't mean the kiss! That was incredible! I mean, something happened to us—to me, at least. I heard your thoughts."

She gaped at him. "What? How can . . . ?"

"I don't know how to explain it. Maybe I imagined it."

Nikki bit her lip. "I don't know what you heard in your mind, but we'll have to discuss it later. The colony's in an uproar, and we need to find Zhao."

Corban was reluctant to let the subject go but knew she was right. "Let's get the truck."

TWENTY-THREE
ROULETTE

Corban led the way back to the barn at a slow jog. Nikki's legs ached, but she did her best to keep up. She didn't think she would be any help overpowering Kun Kaczenski. They skirted the barn, approaching the truck from the back. With the truck's mirrors, she knew there would be no way to surprise the guild master if he was alert.

He wasn't. Kaczenski was in the cab, but he was leaning back in the driver's seat with his eyes closed.

"He's asleep," Corban mouthed, giving her a thumbs-up. He gestured for her to approach the passenger's side. They reached the truck in silence. Nikki saw the rifle resting across Kaczenski's knees and wondered if it was loaded.

Corban held up three fingers. Nikki nodded, understanding. He lowered his fingers one at a time and yanked open the driver's side door the moment he dropped his index finger. He snatched the rifle from Kaczenski's lap and pointed it at his head before the man could react.

"We're borrowing your truck, Mr. Kaczenski." Nikki pointed the sword at him.

The older man's eyes swiveled from Corban to Nikki. He held up his hands in surrender. "Where's the mayor?"

"Dead," Nikki said. "Now get out."

Kaczenski climbed out of the cab, keeping his hands in the air. "Where's Jing?"

Nikki was furious. "You should be asking, 'Where's Zhao?' You're heartless enough to send your own son to Abrams's prison?"

"He's a Stray!" Kaczenski glared at her. "He shouldn't be around Survivors. And it's not a prison! It's an internment fort!"

"That makes it sound so much nicer." She climbed in the passenger's side. "I'm a Stray too! How do you like that fact, you bigot? You had a Stray in your house and didn't even know it!"

Kaczenski's thunderstruck expression gave her no satisfaction. Corban shoved him aside and climbed in the driver's seat, slamming the door in his face.

"You might want to do something about Uncle's body before the bluedeer find him." Corban started the engine. "Personally, I don't care if you bury him or not. It's no more than he deserves."

"The mayor was right! Strays are dangerous! You murdered your own uncle!"

"No, I did!" Nikki reached across Corban and threw the truck into gear. "And we're leaving before I commit another one."

"The colony will hear about it and banish all of you! You'll see!"

Corban floored the accelerator, spraying Kaczenski with dirt from the back tires. He drove to the main road and headed east toward Seventh Fort.

"Foolish man. He's willing to sacrifice his own children for his stupid ideology." Nikki slumped back in the seat, exhausted. "Any bullets in the rifle?"

"No. We'll have to wave it around and look threatening."

Nikki started to giggle but it took too much energy. She leaned her head against the side window and dozed off.

***

A tidal wave of strange memories roused Nikki from a troubled sleep. Startled, she realized Corban reached across the seat to hold her hand as he drove. Her impulse was to pull away but she resisted. *I've been running for too long. I need to learn to control my Talent.*

He peered over. "Sorry. Is the contact overwhelming you?" He tried to let go, but she clung tighter.

"No, wait. I just need to concentrate."

He grinned. "You don't have to shout. I think my hearing's getting better."

"Good." She shut her eyes and put Brida's advice to the test, optimistic from her earlier success during the spontaneous kiss.

It was like editing a holo-vid with a hammer. *Filter out the bad, focus on the good.* In one memory, she saw Leighton raise a hand to slap a younger Corban, but she threw a mental blanket over the scene, and it vanished.

Next, she saw herself through Corban's eyes, sitting in the library at the datafile terminal. He was attracted to her yet terrified at the same time, recalling his premonition. Intrigued, she focused more on this memory. It filled her vision, blocking out the dark images at the fringes of her mind.

It was hard work, but she felt a stirring of confidence. *I can do this, with practice.*

"I heard that." Corban's voice was soft.

Her eyes snapped open. "Heard what?"

"'I can do this, with practice.'"

Nikki pulled her hand away. "How is that possible?"

Corban focused on the road, which was getting rougher by the minute. "I think my empathy has something to do with it. I can sense your emotions without physical contact, but when we touch, I hear an echo of what's in your mind."

"An echo?" Nikki shook her head. "It doesn't make sense."

"When have our Talents ever made sense?" Corban asked. "It is what it is. Brida said we share the same light. Maybe we have some kind of mental connection. Maybe that's what she meant."

"But I can't hear your thoughts. I only see memories."

"Are you sure? Let's try it and see."

"This isn't the time or place to experiment with our Talents."

"It might be important. We need to test it now. Trust me."

He had never asked her that before. She thought of how his trust in her was put to the test an hour ago, when she swung the sword at him. "What should I do?"

"Close your eyes and think of something random." He took her hand again and intertwined his fingers with hers.

Nikki shut her eyes and focused on an ingredient list for a tincture to reduce fever. Corban's memories competed for her attention, but she tried to stay focused. She was getting better at filtering out the negative images coming into her mind. Instead of a flood of memories, it was more like a gentle shower. She imagined herself adding three drops of lavender oil to the pot of water on the stove.

"What are you cooking?" Corban asked.

She gasped and tried to pull her hand away, but he held on.

"Now tell me what I'm thinking."

Nikki shook her head, eyes squeezed shut. "I can't. I only get memories."

"Just try."

The shower became a driving rain, testing her fledgling efforts. Nikki threw up mental blankets to block the dark images of physical pain and humiliation in Corban's past. As she was successful in keeping the darkness at bay, a gentle light began to fill her mind. Without warning, something changed in her consciousness. She experienced it physically, like a static charge. It took her a moment to realize the parade of memories had stopped, yet she was still holding Corban's hand.

What is this? Nikki struggled to remain at this higher level of consciousness she didn't know existed. It took real mental effort to stay focused yet she was eager to explore this strange new world of her Talent. She didn't want to open her eyes or let go of his hand and break the connection.

The light in her mind became brighter. She sensed new emotions that weren't hers, but she didn't have time to evaluate them before she heard a voice. It was like picking up a com and hearing Corban's whisper on the other end. *I just want to kiss you again.*

His external voice, however, said, "There's Seventh Fort. Darkness. It's small."

***

"Thane was right—no windows." Corban pulled off the road and parked the truck behind a cluster of saplings, out of sight of the gates.

Nikki was light-headed. She needed a moment to refocus on reality after being immersed in Corban's mind. She was afraid she wouldn't be able to duplicate her efforts and attain the higher level of consciousness again. *Sixteen storms and I'm just now figuring out my Talent has more than one level.* "Wait, I need a moment."

"What is it? I sensed a lot going on in your mind."

She nodded. "Hard to explain. I need more practice."

Corban got out of the truck. "Unfortunately, it'll have to wait for another time."

She gripped her sword and slipped out of the cab, following him. They found a spot where they could watch the gates without being seen and squatted down in the undergrowth, side by side.

Corban reached for her free hand, but she shook her head. "I need to concentrate. No offense."

"None taken." His tone turned flirtatious. "Some things are worth waiting for."

Nikki blushed. "Let's wait and see what's happening. I wish we could hear what's going on inside."

"Where's Thane when you need him?"

"I hope he's with Jing and Rupert." Nikki focused on the gates to Seventh. The high doors were closed, and two armed soldiers were sitting in folding chairs on either side of the archway.

Five minutes passed before a truck pulled up to the fort with *Potters Guild* painted on the side door. Several people were sitting in the back, but Nikki didn't recognize any of them. The guards opened the gates, the truck drove inside, and they closed the doors behind it.

"We have to get inside and find Zhao," Nikki said. "I think he was hurt when your uncle raided the library."

Corban frowned. "We could try bluffing our way past the guards." He removed the unloaded handgun from his cargo pocket and scowled at it. "They might have bullets in their rifles. We have no way of knowing."

Nikki huffed, impatient. "This is all a stupid game like Russian roulette."

"Russian what?"

"Roulette. One bullet in the chamber. Six people take turns putting the revolver to their heads and pulling the trigger. No one knows who's going to die."

Corban's jaw dropped. "That's a game?"

Nikki shrugged. "Some Earth customs were incredibly stupid."

"Shhhh." Corban pointed to another truck approaching the gates. *Farmers Guild* was painted on the driver's side door.

"Darkness!" Nikki tensed, peering at the profile of the driver. "That's my father."

"How can you tell?"

"He looks like Eliana with a crew cut." Before she took the time to think it through, she was on her feet and moving toward the gates.

"Nikki!" Corban hissed behind her. "What are you doing?"

She looked back at him. "I'm calling their bluff."

Corban scrambled to catch up to her, brandishing his unloaded pistol, for what it was worth.

The guards and Elian Ramirez spotted them at the same time and brought their rifles to bear. "Stop! Put your weapons down!"

"You first, Dad!" Nikki didn't slow her steps.

Her father froze, lowering his rifle a fraction as he climbed from the truck's cab. "What are you doing? Put down the sword, Nikolasa."

"I'm surprised you remember my name." She put all the hatred she could muster into her expression and continued to advance on his position. "Although I'm not surprised you're one of the leaders of the roundup."

As she got closer, she noted a flicker of fear in his eyes. Ilios hadn't been kind to Elian since he spent a great deal of time outside. His face was deeply tanned and etched with wrinkles, making him look older than forty-seven. His gray crew cut exposed a receding hairline. He was hideous to her, both inside and out.

"Put down your weapons!" one of the guards called.

"You first!" She wondered where this brazen courage was coming from.

No one made a move to lower their guns. Nikki stopped two meters from her father but kept her sword ready. "Take the Strays in the truck home. You can't force us to live in this prison."

"You don't know what you're doing." Elian sneered. "Your kind can't live with Normals anymore. You're too dangerous."

"We're being separated from the rest of the colony by force, and you call *us* dangerous?" Corban stepped up next to Nikki and pointed his gun at the guild master. "One woman has already died."

"Lower your weapons," the guard repeated.

"Are you planning to kill us?" Corban asked. "You think that's the solution?"

"Half the colony died from the Plague, but you think Strays need to be locked away too?" Nikki asked.

The guard hesitated.

"Don't listen to them," Elian told the guards. "Take them inside. This is your new home, Nikolasa. Stop trying to act tough with that stupid sword. You know you don't have the courage to use it."

A stinging rebuttal was on the tip of her tongue, but Corban beat her to it. "She used this sword to chop off Abrams's head! Go to the peach orchard and see his body for yourself, if you don't believe me!"

Both guards lowered their rifles. "The mayor's dead?" one of them asked. He looked worried.

"Yes," Nikki said. "Now open the gates and end this madness before someone else dies!"

The asthmatic wheezing of an ancient truck engine reached their ears. No one moved as another vehicle pulled up behind Elian's.

"Corban!" a familiar voice rang out.

Nikki turned to see Thane, Jing, Rupert, and her mother in the back with a few other people she didn't recognize. They all looked as if they had been on the losing side of a battle.

"You're alive!" Relief was evident in every centimeter of Thane's face.

"Mom! What are you doing here?"

"I caught a ride, and now I'm choosing a side." Solona got to her feet and climbed down from the truck. She marched straight over to Elian, taking a stand between him and Nikki like a human shield.

"Solona, I wish I could say it's nice to see you."

"Stop pointing your gun at *my* daughter."

Ramirez responded by shifting the barrel to Solona's forehead. "Shut your mouth. I give the orders here."

"You're a coward. You can only get people to listen if you threaten them with a weapon." Solona's scathing tone made Elian's face turn red.

"I'm warning you to get back! You don't belong here!"

"No one belongs here!" Solona shouted. "This is a prison, and I don't see any criminals here except you!"

"Get back! Don't make me hurt you!"

"You've already hurt me." Solona's tone was acid. "But I won't let you hurt Nikki or any other Stray. Put the gun down and open the gates. The war is over, and you lost."

Nikki watched the heated exchange with a growing sense of dread. She knew her mother wasn't afraid of her father, even with the muzzle of a rifle a decimeter from her forehead, but she sensed Elian was losing control of his anger. *Is his gun loaded?* Solona was betting her life he was bluffing.

"We'll see who's won this war, and who's a coward," Elian said. "You might be unarmed—but he's not."

Before Nikki could blink, her father shifted the rifle so it was pointed at Corban and pulled the trigger.

TWENTY-FOUR
AFTERSHOCK

To Thane, everything happened in slow motion as Ramirez shifted his aim and shot Corban. He watched in horror as his brother gasped and crumpled to the ground, clutching his side. The screams from Nikki, Solona, Jing, and even the gate sentries were so loud, he tuned out his hearing by reflex.

He watched in shock as Solona seized the rifle barrel, yanked the weapon from Ramirez's hands, and swung the stock at his head like a club, knocking him flat. She then dropped to her knees next to Corban and started first aid.

Rupert and Jing scrambled to their feet and pulled Thane up without asking. All three climbed out of the truck and rushed over to the scene. Nikki was hysterical, pressing both hands over the bullet wound to staunch the bleeding. At some point in the confusion, Thane remembered to switch his hearing back on.

"Get him inside!" Solona shouted. "Is there an infirmary?"

"No." One of the gate guards was bending over an unconscious Ramirez. "There's nothing."

"Mom, do something!" Nikki's voice was shrill. "Didn't you bring your kit?"

"It's in the truck." Solona remained calm under pressure. "Jing, get it!"

Everyone was moving fast except Thane. He had witnessed Corban in pain before, no thanks to their sadistic uncle, but this was different. The thought of losing the little brother he looked after his entire life made his blood run cold. Thane became light-headed, his rib gave a sharp throb of pain, and he swallowed the bile rising in his throat.

I'm useless, like Uncle said. I've failed the one person who mattered. I just watched as Ramirez murdered him.

"Thane!" A sharp voice forced him to drag his attention away from the huddle of people surrounding Corban. A small hand gripped his. "Sit down. All the color's drained from your face."

A folding chair was behind him. Jing must have taken it from one of the guards.

"Sit!" When he hesitated, she gripped his forearms and forced him backward into the seat.

"Corban?" Thane hadn't realized his voice could hit such a high register.

"I don't know." Jing was trembling as she pressed close to him, one hand stroking the back of his neck, but he couldn't feel it. He couldn't focus on anything except Corban.

"He needs surgery." Solona's voice was calm, but with a razor-sharp edge to her tone. "The bullet nicked his large intestine. I need four units of O positive blood, a minimum of three saline IVs, and some type of anesthesia, and I need them *right now.*"

215

"There's no beds," one of the sentries said. Both men had abandoned their rifles and were giving Elian Ramirez first aid. The Farmers Guild master was bleeding from a nasty gash on the side of his head. Thane was disappointed he was still breathing.

Nikki stood and looked over at them with an expression that could have melted iron. She wiped her bloody hands on the legs of her jeans as she spoke. "No beds? No infirmary? I suppose there's no working bathrooms or kitchens?"

The sentry who spoke shook his head, eyeing her nervously.

"Did it occur to any of you bigots that Abrams's prison wasn't ready for habitation? Do you think a thousand people can live in a fort that's nothing more than a barn?" Her voice cracked with sarcasm. "Did you spread hay on the floors for us to sleep on, or is that expecting too much?"

"There's a well," the other sentry said with a touch of defiance. "Supplies can be trucked in."

"Until the trucks wear out, which should be any day now," Rupert said.

"We're not staying here." Nikki scanned the faces of the small crowd assembled in front of the gates. "Abrams is dead, so this ends now."

Uncle is dead? Thane felt a spark of hope at her words.

"The Strays agreed to come to prevent any more bloodshed," Jing said.

"How's that plan working out?" Thane noted the brittle edge in Nikki's tone. He sympathized with anyone foolish enough to cross her.

"Whether we stay or not, we can't move Corban," Solona said. "He's losing too much blood, and I need

216

to operate on him *immediately* so someone sure as darkness better get a room set up for surgery!"

"I'll send a message to the nearest surgeon," Rupert said. "I need a name."

"Lorna DeKalb," Solona said, "Waterfall. Tell her to bring every surgical supply she can get her hands on. And tell her to hurry."

"Yes, ma'am." Rupert shut his eyes. "Message sent."

Thane reached out to grasp Jing's hand on his shoulder, grateful for her presence.

"Let's get him inside." Solona eyed Rupert, and he hurried to assist her.

"I can help." Thane tried to stand, but Jing seized his shoulders and kept him in the chair.

"Let Solona take care of him." Her dark eyes sparkled with tears, but her tone was firm. "And I'll take care of you."

Thane was too emotionally exhausted to argue.

TWENTY-FIVE
INTERNMENT

Nikki was worried Corban's wound would get infected. Although she was a firm believer in the medicinal properties of herbs, a single shot of antibiotics would have put her mind at ease, but there wasn't any left in the colony. She had asked her mother several times if they could move him to the hospital ship or at least the infirmary in Waterfall, but the answer was always no.

"He's too weak to move," Solona said. "Dr. DeKalb did a good job with the surgery. He'll make a full recovery."

"But he's not getting better in this filthy place!"

"Primitive isn't the same thing as filthy," Solona said. "He has everything he needs here, and Dr. DeKalb brings new IVs and bandages every day. He'll heal, be patient." Her mother went back to mixing a poultice in the mortar and pestle she managed to acquire from a truckload of supplies from the Herbalists Guild. The fact that she was sitting cross-legged on the floor to work didn't seem to bother her.

Nikki didn't share her optimism. She helped Solona change Corban's bandages every day and rub healing oils over the stitches keeping his wounds closed. The bullet had passed through his right side, below his ribcage, miraculously missing his liver but leaving a large exit wound in his back. With his torn oblique muscles, Corban wouldn't be able to lift anything heavy with his right arm again or even raise his arm over his head to swing a machete. His Hunters Guild days were over, although Nikki knew he would be pleased to hear the news when he was fully awake.

She couldn't believe her father pulled the trigger. What did he have to gain by shooting Corban? *Mom's right. He's a coward.* She hadn't seen Elian since they moved Corban inside the fort to the make-shift surgical/recovery room in the east wall, and she hoped to never see him again.

Corban's hospital bed was the only piece of furniture in Seventh. Nikki, Solona, and Jing slept in blankets on the floor of his room. Solona had administered the last IV yesterday, so now the three women took turns getting him to drink nutrient-infused water every two hours to keep him hydrated. Nikki emptied his urinary catheter bag twice a day, although she knew Corban would be mortified to learn this fact.

Thane, Rupert, and Zhao were regular visitors. They slept in a room across the hall. The fortress didn't have any apartments, only individual rooms. In Nikki's mind, it was designed to be a prison, and no one could persuade her otherwise.

"Solona, sorry to bother you." Thane stuck his head in the door, midmorning on seventh-day. "But could you check my rib? The wrapping's shifted, and it really hurts."

"Yes, but you'll have to stand." Solona dug a clean roller bandage out of her kit and motioned him inside. Zhao took Thane's place in the doorway, nodding a greeting to each person in the room.

Jing sat up on her bedroll and watched with wide-eyed interest as Thane took off his T-shirt, one-handed. Nikki was tempted to tell her to stop drooling. She perched next to Corban on the bed, careful not to disturb him. He slept a great deal but was waking more often and sounding more coherent each time he woke.

"Do you think we can go back to Lakeside when Corban's recovered?" Jing asked Solona when she finished wrapping Thane's chest.

"You don't have to wait," Thane said. "You or Solona, you're not Strays."

"We're all colonists." Jing's tone turned sulky. "We're in this together. Stop trying to make me leave."

"I'm not—" Thane began, but she cut him off with a sob. "Jing—"

"Come on, Jing." Nikki tried to sound soothing, but her friend was already vacating the room in tears.

Thane grabbed his shirt and limped after her.

"She's exhausted," Solona called. "She'll calm down. Give her time."

"We're all exhausted," Zhao said. "But I'm not allowed to sleep because I have a concussion."

"Your recovery time is over," Solona told him. "You can sleep now."

"I saw the bullet hole in the bathroom door," Nikki said. "You're lucky they missed."

The sound of sobbing returned, but it was an infant's cry.

"I can't get Travis to settle down." Eliana hovered in the doorway, swaying her bundle of joy from side to side in her arms.

"There's a lot going on," Solona said.

"It's quiet in our room. I think something else is bothering him."

"Can he sense emotions, like Corban?" Nikki asked.

"I think it's deeper than that," Eliana said. "It's like he can tell when something bad's about to happen."

"Something bad already happened," Zhao said.

"Something bad is still happening," Nikki said. "We can't stay here. Do they expect us to live like animals?" She put her hand on Corban's forehead. *Yes, he's awake.*

"Are you sure it's safe for you to touch him?" Solona asked.

"I told you I'm able to sift through memories now and block out the bad ones," Nikki said. "At least I can with Corban. We have some kind of mental connection."

"I don't understand—"

"Brida Vaughn told us we share the same light, and she was right. She had an incredible Talent, more powerful than any of us." Nikki wrestled with her growing impatience. She had explained this to her mother twice. "You don't have to understand it, Mom. Just accept it. I had a breakthrough with my Talent, and I intend to learn how to use it, with Corban's help."

"How can he help you if he's unconscious?" Eliana asked.

"He's awake." Nikki smiled. "He's trying to open his eyes."

Right on cue, and because he was listening, Corban's eyelids fluttered open.

"See? What did I tell you?" Nikki sensed something was wrong. "He's going to be sick! Help me, Zhao!"

Zhao hastened to obey, and he and Nikki rolled Corban onto his left side. A basin was ready but she was surprised at how much his empty stomach produced.

"It's probably a reaction to the last dose of morphine," Solona said. "Get the peppermint and ginger oils from my bag."

"Yes, ma'am." Nikki and Zhao eased Corban onto his back when he finished vomiting. As soon as Nikki dug the two vials of essential oil from her mother's tote bag, Thane and Jing were back, and they were both out of breath.

"Solona! They need you upstairs!" Thane said.

"In a minute. I'm taking care of your brother," she snapped, frustrated.

"Robin Aziz is in labor!" Jing announced. "Her husband thinks the baby's breech!"

Solona swore. "Nikki, take over here. Jing, get my bag."

Everyone except Zhao left in a hurry, and he only lingered long enough to ask, "Can I do anything else to help?"

"Thanks, but I've got it covered. I'm sure Mom could use your help finding towels or fetching a bucket of water from the well."

"Got it. See you later."

The sudden silence was unnerving. Nikki observed Corban, who was opening his eyes again. "You sure you want to do that?"

"I wanted to make sure you weren't disgusted with me."

"I cut off your uncle's head." She covered the basin with a towel and moved it to a corner of the room so they wouldn't smell it. "Cleaning up a little vomit is a pleasant holiday, in comparison."

Corban almost chuckled, but it turned into a grimace. He put a hand on his bandaged side. "I guess I'm going to live?"

"Yes." She sat next to him and wiped his mouth with a damp cloth. "Sorry, it's cold."

"It's fine, thank you. You know, I've never been taken care of by such an attractive nurse."

Nikki raised an eyebrow at him. "You think it's attractive I'm wearing the same blood-stained clothes and haven't washed my hair in four days?"

"You look good to me."

She wondered if it was the morphine talking. "I don't think I smell very good."

"That's just my puke breath. You smell fine. What have I missed since I've been unconscious?"

Nikki wasn't sure where to start, so she sidestepped the question. She opened the bottle of ginger oil. "Are you ticklish?" She moved to the foot of the bed and uncovered his feet.

"No, and why?" Corban watched with interest as she applied a few drops of oil to the soles of his feet and massaged them.

Nikki struggled to resist the wave of memories which threatened to distract her from her task. "It's for nausea."

"How is putting it on my feet going to make my stomach feel better?"

"It's absorbed into your bloodstream. There are pressure points on the feet—" She stopped explaining when he laughed. "You said you weren't ticklish."

"I didn't think I was. Maybe I'm laughing because I've never had a beautiful woman massage my feet."

Definitely the morphine talking.

"I heard that," Corban said.

Nikki rolled her eyes at him and applied a few drops of the peppermint oil. She continued to massage his feet, and he continued to laugh.

"Darkness. It hurts," he said between chuckles.

"Sorry." She took her hands off his feet and breathed a mental sigh of relief at the sudden quiet in her mind.

"No, the massage doesn't hurt, the laughing does. You don't have to stop."

"I don't want you to pull out your stitches."

Corban's expression turned serious. "You didn't answer my question. What's happened since I've been in dreamland?"

"Day one—you were in surgery." Nikki perched on the side of the bed but was careful not to touch him to keep her mind clear. "Dr. DeKalb from Waterfall knows mom well. She showed up with a truck full of medical supplies and they put you back together. Day two—the Strays woke up and realized they were living in a barn. The interior of the fort's not finished but your uncle didn't care if we had the basic necessities before banishing us. Days two and three—we dug latrines, hauled water from the well, and cooked over open fires, but this isn't camping. The Strays came without resistance after Brida's

224

death, except for the ones in Lakeside, which is still on lockdown."

"Won't they starve?"

"No, Mom says it's business as usual, except the gates are closed and Brooks personally monitors everyone who comes and goes. Shipments of food are delivered here every day, although the rest of the colony figured out they're understaffed now and have to work longer hours. Mom says Brooks is going to see us restored to our homes as soon as tensions settle down."

"Tensions?"

Nikki shrugged, frowning. "There were lots of injuries during the roundup. Families were torn apart. The colony's still in chaos."

"Lots of deaths?"

"No, just the two." Nikki turned her face toward the window. "Almost three," she added in a soft voice.

"Have you gotten any sleep since I was shot?"

She shook her head, not meeting his gaze, but then she grinned and turned to look at him. "Before you ask—yes, once I tried curling up next to you, but I couldn't shut off the flood of memories to fall sleep."

"I hate to think you've worn yourself out worrying over me."

"You almost bled to death. If my mother hadn't been right there—" A tear leaked from the corner of each eye, but Nikki wiped them away on her sleeve.

"Did she really knock out your dad with his own rifle? Remind me to never make her mad." Corban was attempting to sound flippant, but it came off as flat.

"I'll never let anyone hurt you again," Nikki said. "You were abused your whole life, and I promise those days are over." She leaned over and kissed him on the cheek. "I'll kiss you again, properly, after we've both brushed our teeth."

Corban studied her face with a thoughtful expression. "You're dead on your feet. Want to give sleep another try?" He extended his left arm and wiggled his eyebrows at her. "Plenty of room right here."

Nikki knew it wouldn't work, but she humored him by lying down in the narrow space at his left. He curled his arm around her shoulders and kissed her on the forehead.

"Want some covers?"

"No!" She said it louder than she intended. "Don't lift your blanket. You've got nothing on."

"What?" Corban turned his head to the right and peeked under the covers. "Darkness!" His face turned pink. "Have you seen me naked?"

"No! I swear, nothing below the belt." Her own cheeks burned.

"I'm not wearing a belt." Corban laughed again, wincing with each chuckle. "It's fine. I can sense you're telling the truth."

Nikki shut her eyes and sifted through his memories. She was getting better at blocking the unpleasant ones, but was unable to reach the higher level of consciousness. It was frustrating. *It'd be nice to stay here and not have to deal with the mental overload.*

"I agree." Corban held her closer for a moment. "You need sleep." He nudged her out of the bed. "You can practice your Talent on me another time."

"Someone needs to keep an eye on you." Nikki gave him a half-hearted pout. "Especially while you've got morphine in your system."

"You think this is the morphine talking?" Corban grinned. "This is the real me, angel."

"Angel? You sound like a bad holo-vid. Now I know it's the morphine." She reluctantly went over to her bedroll. "But you're right. I'm exhausted."

"Thane will hear me if I need anything. Go to sleep," Corban said.

Nikki lay back on her pillow and allowed herself to close her eyes.

***

It was dark when she woke. Solona, Jing, and Corban were asleep in the room. Nikki sat up, too uncomfortable to sleep with a full bladder and an empty stomach. She stood, stretched, and stepped to the window.

The courtyard was deserted. The dying embers of dozens of cooking fires bathed the grounds in dim, flickering light. A tented-off area near the main gates sheltered the latrines. She frowned but knew her other option was a bedpan. She found her shoes and tiptoed out of the room.

She ran into Zhao outside the door with an oil lamp in his hand. "Why are you up?" he whispered.

"I was going to ask you the same thing."

"I went to sleep as soon as Solona gave me the word."

"Same here, only it was Corban who told me to get some sleep."

"This is a fascinating conversation, but I have to visit the latrine, so if you'll excuse me." Zhao turned toward the stairs.

"Me too. Let me walk with you, I need the light." She fell into step beside him. "Did Robin Aziz have her baby?"

"Yes. Thane and I waited in the hallway and heard a newborn crying right at dusk. I was too tired to stick around for the celebration."

"How can anyone celebrate here?" Nikki pushed open the door to the courtyard. "Did the poor woman at least have a bed for the delivery?"

"A mattress on the floor, I was told."

"Darkness. That's awkward—as if childbirth wasn't painful enough."

Zhao grunted, clearly not interested in discussing the topic any further.

Nikki was quiet as they made their way across the dirt courtyard, skirting fire pits and tables cobbled together with scrap lumber. She peered at each table they passed, hoping to find something leftover to eat. She picked up two carrots and offered one to Zhao.

He sighed. "Better than nothing."

They reached the latrine, which was divided into two spaces for privacy. Nikki ducked beneath the awning to the women's side. An oil lamp burned on a scrap wood table, next to a basin filled with semi-clean water. There was a cake of soap on the table. She squatted over the disgusting latrine, threw a shovelful of dirt over the smelly contents of the ditch, and scrubbed her face and hands at the basin. *If only I had a towel and some clean clothes to change into.* She made up her mind to locate both and come back as soon as possible.

Nikki emerged from the restroom to find Zhao waiting for her with the lamp. "Ready?" He munched his carrot and started across the courtyard.

"We're not staying in Seventh." Nikki hurried to catch up to him. "These conditions are intolerable."

"I don't think there's anything we can do about it right now." Zhao dropped his carrot top on the ground. "The rest of the colony's in turmoil. Eventually, they'll get desperate enough to want us back."

Nikki raised an eyebrow at him. "You think your father will ask you to come home?"

Zhao snorted. "Never, but he'll want Jing back."

"My father probably wishes he had a Normal child too."

"At least you have your mother. I like to imagine my mother would've wanted me around."

Nikki was tempted to pat him on the back, but she resisted, reluctant to deal with a fresh wave of dark memories. "You'll have a family of your own someday."

"I don't know," Zhao whispered, slowing his steps.

Nikki stopped walking. "What's wrong?"

Zhao turned to face her, his expression troubled. The lamp-light bathed half his face in flickering shadow. "Corban's last premonition, the night before the roundup."

"He had another dream?" Nikki ran the tip of her tongue over dry lips. "He didn't mention it to me."

"He probably didn't have a chance to tell you before he was shot." Zhao took a deep breath. "He said there was an explosion and the whole landing strip was on fire."

"What exploded? I don't understand."

"Neither does he, but he said it was the end of the colony."

A painful knot formed in Nikki's stomach, displacing her hunger pains. "An important detail is always missing from his premonitions. How did he know it was the end?"

Zhao frowned. "He sounded certain."

"A fire at the landing strip couldn't destroy the forts." Nikki tried to think. "I need to see that dream. I need to be sure."

"Jing told me you can't see memories in any particular order. How're you going to single out one from Corban's mind?"

"You could teach me." Nikki peered into his face, so similar to his sister's, and mustered a hopeful smile. "Please?"

"Our Talents are different. I don't know how I can help you."

"How did you learn to control yours?"

Zhao shrugged and resumed their walk. "I practiced. I held an object for hours and sifted through the impressions I got until I was able to make sense of it."

Nikki frowned. "It's mentally exhausting for me to have contact with Corban for more than a few minutes."

"I don't know what to suggest." Zhao held the door to the stairs for her. "I'm sorry."

They reached the second floor and their respective rooms. "Thanks anyway," Nikki said. "Goodnight, Zhao."

"'Night." He extinguished the lamp and closed the door to his room.

Nikki shut the door to Corban's room and leaned her back against it, waiting for her eyes to adjust to the darkness. Her emotions were in turmoil. According to Zhao, something more horrible than the internment was coming, something Corban thought was the end of the colony.

Corban didn't see his uncle in the orchard. He didn't know I was coming to rescue him, not kill him. There's always a missing detail in his premonitions. Another set of eyes might see it from a different perspective. I need to see that dream.

She rubbed her forehead, grappling with her limited knowledge of her Talent. *I can edit memories, blocking the bad ones and focusing on the good, and I've learned to control the speed they come at me. But I don't know how to put them in chronological order, and I don't know how to locate a specific memory. What am I doing wrong?*

Brida said I have to choose what I want to see. A new idea took shape. *Could I ask Corban to recall a specific memory?* She knew she needed to reach the higher level of consciousness she experienced while they were in the truck, but she hadn't been able to duplicate the feat a second time. Reflecting on it four days later, she worried it had just been an accident, and she wouldn't be able to reach it again.

Corban can hear my thoughts, through his empathic Talent. How did he describe it? Like hearing an echo? Nikki thought she needed hours of practice, like Zhao, to master the higher level of consciousness. Could she be connected to Corban's mind for hours without it causing him or her some kind of mental damage?

Why do I feel like I'm taking a final exam after missing a class the entire semester? She stared down at Corban and made a decision. *I have to try.*

She stepped over to his bed and lay down on his left side, facing him, staying as quiet as possible. He stirred, but she put a hand over his mouth. *Shhhh, don't speak. It's not very private in here.*

TWENTY-SIX
SHARED LIGHT

Corban suspected his empathic Talent had somehow intensified since the shooting. Even half-asleep, he sensed when Nikki was near, but physical contact enabled him to hear her thoughts as easily as hearing a voice on the other end of a com. It was strange yet exhilarating at the same time. For the first time in his life, he didn't hate his modified DNA.

He understood that their mental communication didn't come easily for Nikki. Her Talent for seeing memories was an unusual area of telepathy, and she needed time to learn to control it. Corban assumed she would wait until he fully healed before trying again to reach what she described as a 'higher level of consciousness' which allowed her to hear his thoughts.

But when she cuddled up next to him in the middle of the night, he was wide awake and pleasantly surprised. *I can't hear your thoughts, so I need you to please be patient for a few minutes,* she thought. *Actually, I don't know how long it will take. Sorry to keep you awake.*

In response, he lifted the hand she placed over his mouth, turned it over, and kissed her knuckles.

That's not helping!

He shook with silent laughter as she snatched her hand away.

I want to try an experiment.

He bobbed his chin once to let her know he understood.

Thank you. Her mind was busy for a time and Corban tried to relax. It was hard for him to envision what she was doing. He was aware of dark images, uncomfortable memories from his past, but she refused to allow any of them to take shape. It was like his mind was a stage and she was a stage-hand, busy moving scenery into the wings. Whenever she succeeded in getting one piece of scenery off-stage, another one rolled in to take its place, but she persisted. He wondered if it was as mentally exhausting for her as it would be for someone physically clearing a stage of heavy backdrops.

At last she managed to clear the stage of his mind, and he became aware of a soft light filling the empty space, like a spotlight. The light grew brighter. He sensed her triumph as she embraced the light. It was as if she picked up a com, and now they were able to communicate without speaking.

This takes a lot of concentration for me, she thought, *so try not to think about anything else.*

All right. He was intrigued but made an effort not to ask any questions.

I need you to show me your last premonition, the one about the fire at the landing strip.

Corban winced. *How did you—?*

Don't distract me. Her tone was sharp. *Please think back to your dream. Show it to me.*

234

She was asking to see a specific memory. Was this possible, and why did she want to see it?

Please, I'm losing focus. He sensed her frustration.

Corban relented, going back to the dream in his mind. It took more effort than he expected to envision his own memory, but he realized that was the nature of memories. They could be seen, heard, and interpreted differently each time they were revisited. He tried to remove his own bias from the dream to allow her to come to her own conclusion, if, in fact, she saw and heard what he experienced.

Show me again. She sounded uncertain.

Corban felt a headache coming on. It was the first time their shared connection exacted a toll on his mind. He thought of the premonition again—the explosion, the fire, the smoke, and the sense of foreboding he was unable to explain.

Nikki abruptly got up from the bed, severing their connection.

Corban opened his eyes and looked up at her standing over him in the darkness. Her fear was palpable. "What did you see?" he whispered.

"I saw a strange ship, before the explosion. There were twenty ships on the landing strip."

TWENTY-SEVEN
THANE'S DILEMMA

Thane missed the privacy, space, and working bathroom of the library ship. He even missed his room in Uncle's apartment, which was vacant now. He and Corban would have a place to live, if West Fort allowed them to return.

He had read in Earth's history about ethnic cleansings, where countries drove out and slaughtered people they deemed inferior because they were a different bloodline, race, or religion. To exile the Strays for the crime of being different through no fault of their own was cruel, and being forced to live in primitive Seventh Fort was adding insult to injury.

Despite the uncomfortable living conditions, Thane was more concerned about Corban. Although he was grateful to Solona Zegarelli and Lorna DeKalb for taking care of Corban after the shooting, Thane thought his brother needed to be in the hospital ship to make a full recovery. Thane's own injury was uncomfortable, but he considered it a temporary inconvenience, unlike his leg, which was a permanent inconvenience.

Then there was Jing. Thane couldn't decide if she was temporary or permanent. He suspected her sudden romantic interest in him was a way of coping with the shock of recent events.

On the fifth day after the roundup, he was awakened by a message from Derek. *The sentry told me Kun Kaczeski's at the gates. He wants to talk to Jing.*

Thane was too sleepy to figure out why Derek didn't send Jing the message. He sat up and looked around the dimly lit room he shared with Zhao and Rupert. Since the exterior rooms were windowless, Thane classified their three-by-three meter space as a prison cell. The rooms with windows facing the courtyard weren't any better except for the additional light.

He found his brace, strapped it on, and pulled on his boots before struggling to his feet. Between his left leg and his right ribcage, getting up from the floor was a real challenge.

Thane slipped out the door and crossed the hallway to Corban's room. He tapped on the door before poking his head in and surveying the arrangement of slumbering bodies. Corban was in the middle, lying on the only bed, surrounded on three sides by his guardian angels curled up in blankets. Solona, Jing, and Nikki took up most of the room's floor space. No one was resting comfortably.

Thane stepped inside and went over to Jing, prodding her gently with his foot. He noted a pair of pants on the floor near her feet and hoped she was wearing pajamas.

Her eyes popped open, and she sat up with a dimpled smile. "Good morning."

He put a finger to his lips, cautioning her to be quiet.

She nodded and got to her feet, but he averted his gaze when he caught a glimpse of bare legs outside her blanket.

Jing giggled. "Just a second." He heard the rustling of clothes and a zipper before she took his hand. "I'm ready."

He led her out of the room, shut the door, and turned to face her, but she was already on tiptoes, attempting to reach his mouth with hers. "Wait." Thane caught her by the shoulders and took a step back.

Jing glared at him without heat. She made an effort to kiss him at least twice a day since the roundup, but he managed to dodge every attempt. "Is it my breath? It's my morning breath, isn't it?"

"No," he said for the umpteenth time. "I don't want to kiss you yet. Please don't rush me."

"Why did you wake me up then?" Jing's pout reminded him she was three storms younger than he was. She didn't seem mature enough for a serious relationship, so he made every effort to dial back her romantic interest in him to 'just friends.' So far it wasn't working.

"Your father wants to talk to you."

Jing frowned. "I don't have anything to say to him, not after he banished Zhao and was going to let your uncle shoot Corban—after watching him murder Brida Vaughn!"

"Maybe he's seen the error of his ways?"

"Too little, too late," Jing said. "If he's come seeking my forgiveness, he's wasting his breath."

Thane took her elbow and steered her toward the stairs. "Why don't you see what he has to say? It can't hurt."

Jing made a scathing noise, but allowed Thane to lead her downstairs to the courtyard. They walked past cooking fires, where a few early-risers were preparing breakfast, and headed toward the gates.

Derek met them in front of the high doors. He was bouncing his inconsolable son in his arms.

"I can't believe you haven't taken your family back to Lakeside," Thane blurted out before taking time to reconsider his words. "This is no place for an infant."

Derek shrugged. "Eliana wants to keep the family together. As long as Solona and Nikki are here, she'll stay. Besides, my Talent's needed to contact people outside Seventh."

"My father wants to see me?" Jing interrupted their debate with a scowl.

Derek nodded, lifting Travis to his shoulder and patting him on the back. "He's right outside."

"Do you want me to go with you?" Thane hoped the answer was no. He wasn't eager to witness any Kaczenski family drama. The Herbalists Guild master had treated him, Corban, and his own son with such contempt, Thane knew his presence wouldn't be welcomed.

"No, just make sure he doesn't try to take me back to Lakeside." Jing tugged on the iron handle to one of the doors. "I wouldn't be surprised if that's what he has in mind."

The door opened enough for her to slip outside, and she pulled it shut behind her.

Derek and Thane regarded each other with concerned frowns, and it dawned on Thane why

Nikki's brother-in-law summoned him. "I'm going to step over here." Thane eyed Travis with sympathy. The baby's face was red from crying. "So I can hear better."

Derek nodded, giving him a thumbs-up with his free hand.

Thane walked a dozen paces away from the gates to an empty spot in the courtyard. He shut his eyes and listened.

"*Baba.*" Jing's tone was cool. "Why are you here?"

"I want you to come home. You don't belong with these people." Kun Kaczenski was making an effort to sound contrite.

"I told you if you sent Zhao away, I'd leave too."

"Nonsense! You're not a Stray, and you're not of age to defy my wishes! Come home with me right now!"

Thane raised an eyebrow. *That didn't take long.*

"You chose to follow a bad man who wanted to imprison all the Strays. Are you happy with the results? Do you think Brida Vaughn deserved to die?"

"I saw it happen. It was an accident," Kun stammered.

"Nikki told me he was aiming for Corban when he fired the gun. You chose to support a man who wanted to murder his own nephew, a man who imprisoned an entire group of people because they're different. I have no stomach for your prejudice, *Baba.* You disgust me."

That was harsh, but accurate. Thane shifted his feet, wondering if the guild master was thinking up any new arguments.

"It was a mistake," Kun whispered. "Forgive me."

"It's too late! Look at this terrible place! Look what you've done to the colony!"

"How . . . how is your brother?" Thane was sure this new tactic wouldn't work.

"You're asking me about Zhao, after what you've done to him? Do you think he deserves to be here, in exile?"

"I want to see him," Kun said. "I want to tell him I'm sorry."

"Go away, *Baba*. You've done enough damage already. You deserve to be alone."

Thane heard the gate door creak and turned to see Jing slip back inside the fort. Unshed tears filled her eyes but her face was bright red with anger. He walked over to her, intending to offer a word of support, but she threw her arms around his waist and buried her face in his sternum. His rib gave a twinge of pain but he ignored it as he held her. Her body shook with sobs.

Thane pondered his dilemma. He wanted to respond to Jing's desire for closeness, but he envisioned it leading to more pain for both of them down the road. When the current crisis was over, she would realize he was just a convenient warm body, ill-equipped to be a life partner. He already knew he was attracted to her because she was the first woman to show any interest in him, but they didn't have the kind of spark Corban and Nikki shared. Jing didn't need to waste her affections on a worthless cripple.

I need to distance myself. It'll be less painful in the long run. She'll probably hate me, but I can live with that if it means she'll find real joy later with the right person.

Jing kept bawling, so Thane resolved to be patient. He scanned nearby conversations and overheard two Tailors Guild Strays arguing in the men's latrine.

"We should stay," the first young man said. "We could finish building the fort. We knew this was coming. The Survivors have treated us like vermin since the Plague."

"No, this is wrong," the second said. "This place isn't fit for animals, and we're members of the colony. They need us."

"They've made it clear they don't want us. Why go back to that?"

"Being forced to live in exile is worse than being called a worthless Stray once in a while. I'll take my chances and live with the bigots."

"I say we start our own settlement. They need us, but we don't need them. With our Talents we could turn this place into a palace."

"With no electricity?" The second man became agitated. "No plumbing? The colony doesn't have the resources to provide anything else for us here. We're lucky they've trucked in food. Can you imagine if they forced us here before the storm? We'd starve."

Thane heard water splashing. "Coward," the first man said. "You're afraid of living rough after being pampered in Greenfield all your life?"

"This isn't living rough. This is living like animals. You know Abrams had no intention of running electricity here."

Yes, it all comes back to Uncle. Thane debated listening for a few more minutes when Travis let out a piercing scream.

Jing raised her face from Thane's damp T-shirt, and they both turned to stare at Derek and the baby. Nikki's brother-in-law appeared helpless to comfort his screaming child.

"Summon Elaina." Thane thought Travis was in extreme pain.

242

Derek nodded.

And then Thane heard it. He looked up into the sky, straining his Talent to hear over Travis's screams. The far-off roar was coming closer, descending on the colony.

"What is it?" Jing followed his gaze. "What do you hear?"

"It sounds like engines." Thane couldn't see anything, but the sound was getting closer.

What do you hear? Derek asked.

A glint of metal reflecting off Ilios in the northern sky caught Thane's eye. He was speechless for a moment as the shape grew, coming closer to Vesta. "It's a ship."

TWENTY-EIGHT
SHIP

"Listen to me!" Solona climbed up on the bed of a produce truck. "I have news!"

"You're going to have to yell louder, Mom." Nikki looked over the crowd of Strays that filled the courtyard. She scanned the additional faces at the windows overlooking the square, faces filled with excitement and apprehension.

News of the ship spread fast. People were eager to get to the landing strip to greet the new arrivals and see what supplies Earth sent the colony after the sixteen-storm absence. Now it was midday, and the Strays were growing impatient.

Nikki climbed up beside Solona and put two fingers in her mouth, whistling loud to get people's attention.

The chatter died down.

"Rupert Conquist's at the landing strip, and he sent me word about the ship!" Solona shouted.

The crowd fell silent, straining to hear.

"It's a small ship, and it touched down near the library, but the airlock's remained shut. The five mayors and their delegations waited outside all morning, but there's been no communication from the ship's crew. We're not sure if it's unmanned or the occupants are in stasis. We'll have to wait until someone comes out, or the Mechanics Guild master will open the airlock in a few days if no one does."

A few people booed. "That's not good enough!" someone shouted.

"Be patient!" Solona bellowed. "As soon as the ship's open, they'll send us word."

"Any supplies are rightfully ours!" another person shouted. "The Survivors can't expect us to live in these conditions! We need solar panels and tools!"

"We need beds!" a woman yelled. "And bathrooms!"

"Be patient!" Nikki added her voice to her mother's, although she didn't expect her words to placate the crowd. She regarded Zhao, standing near the tailgate. His face reflected her anxiety.

Only the team knew about Corban's premonition. Nikki was convinced anyone who went near the landing strip might be killed if the ship turned out to be a curse instead of a blessing as Corban foresaw.

"Go back to work!" Solona shouted. "Rupert will send me a message as soon as the airlock opens!"

Grumbling, the crowd dispersed. Strays and the few dozen friends or family members like Solona and Jing, who went into exile with them, returned to their tasks of making Seventh Fort more livable.

Nikki and her mother climbed down from the truck bed, so the driver could head back to Greenfield.

Solona had biked to Lakeside with Rupert earlier in the day to ensure his safe passage to the landing strip. She told Nikki Survivors were too distracted by the arrival of the ship to care if Strays left Seventh.

"If we can leave, let's do it," Nikki said. "Corban's strong enough to move. He'll heal better in Lakeside's infirmary."

"We'll see." Solona frowned. "We'll have to convince one of the guilds to let us use their truck. Right now, they seem happier to have us out of the way."

Nikki was forced to swallow her impatience, like everyone else. She walked to Dagmar Piroux's cooking station and ladled a bowl of steaming chicken broth from the large cast-iron pot suspended over the fire.

"I haven't added the vegetables yet." Dagmar looked over from the rickety table where she was dicing potatoes.

"It's for Corban," Nikki said.

Dagmar nodded. "Ask him if he's up for bread this evening. Poor guy has to be starving on a liquid diet."

"I will, thanks." Nikki carried the bowl up to Corban's room.

"Lunch is served." She was surprised to see no one else in the room. "I thought Jing was supposed to be taking care of you."

Corban was sitting up in bed, pillows propped behind him. "She was until Thane came by a few minutes ago." He grinned. "I think she was a bit distracted."

Nikki perched next to him on the bed. "Distracted, why? She said Thane's been doing his best to discourage her. Are you feeling strong enough to feed yourself?"

"Yes, please." Corban took the spoon from her. "Although you should probably hold the bowl. I'm not sure if Thane wants to discourage her or not."

Nikki held the bowl close to his chin so he was able to get the spoon to his mouth without dripping hot broth onto his chest. "He needs to make up his mind. It's not fair to Jing."

"There's a lot of unfairness going on right now." Corban caught her eye and paused, empty spoon in mid-air. "For example, I think it's fair to assume you'll get tired of taking care of me, and tired of our weird mental connection."

Nikki felt as if she took an unexpected plunge into Gray Lake. "Is that what you think?" The words came out sharper than she intended.

Corban's countenance fell at her response. He looked worried for all of five seconds until she set the bowl on the floor and cupped his face in her hands, leaning in for a long kiss which raised the temperature of the room by several degrees.

Is that what you think of me? She ignored the memories, forcing them to the fringes of her mind, and concentrated on pouring her positive emotions into the kiss, determined to leave no doubt in Corban's mind of how she felt about him.

"Is this some kind of new treatment the Herbalists Guild's trying out?" Zhao's voice interrupted from the doorway. "If so, sign me up!"

Nikki broke off the marathon kiss and glared over her shoulder at the source of the rude interruption. "Don't you know how to knock?"

Zhao laughed. "The door's wide open, Nurse Ramirez." He slouched into the room and sat cross-legged on the floor near the foot of the bed. "Seriously, though, I'm looking for Thane."

"He's off somewhere with your sister," Corban said.

"Not the kind of thing a *ge'-ge'* wants to hear."

Nikki ignored his teasing. "Why do you need to see him?"

"Because Rupert contacted me, and I need Thane's advice." Zhao's grin faded. "My father's requested I come to the landing strip. Seems they need my help to determine who sent the ship."

"No!" Nikki said it without thinking. "It's too dangerous."

Zhao peered over at Corban. "I know—the premonition."

"Then you understand why you can't go," Corban said. "I'm already worried Rupert's too close."

"But the explosion doesn't happen until you're at the bridge, right?" Zhao asked. "It could be weeks or months from now."

"I don't know." Corban exchanged a worried frown with Nikki. "A piece of the puzzle's missing, and it's usually a critical piece of information."

"Now Kun wants your help?" Nikki balled her hands into fists. "Suddenly he decides your Talent's useful? What a hypocrite."

"Maybe it's a good thing," Zhao said. "Maybe it'll help bridge the gap Abrams created with the internment. If the Survivors recognize our Talents are useful, we could exchange our services for supplies."

"That's assuming we stay here." Nikki frowned.

Zhao shrugged. "It's better than relying on their reluctant charity to survive, or waiting for them to come to their senses and allow us to return home."

Nikki knew he had a point, but she wasn't interested in turning their prison into a home. She *had* a home and wanted to go back to it as soon as possible. "If you feel like you should help your father, why do you need Thane's advice?"

"I thought his Talent might be more useful in this situation," Zhao said. "He could hear if anyone inside the ship's still alive."

ACKNOWLEDGEMENTS

Thank you to the wonderful people who helped make this book a reality. First, to my family, who have always been supportive of the time and privacy I need to write. Second, to my beta readers, authors Lisa Rector, Tamara Ward, and CS Johnson. Third, to my cover artist Jessica Phillips, who was able to turn photographer Rylee Jensen's work into a masterpiece, and to my cover models, Jared Weaver, Jayden Beach, and Aaron Weaver. Fourth, to my map artist, author Cindy Clark, and finally a big thank you to my editors Laura Walker and Lisa Rector.

SterlingRWalker.com

www.ingramcontent.com/pod-product-compliance
Lightning Source LLC
Chambersburg PA
CBHW061610170626
46811CB00001B/381